A CONARD
COUNTY BABY

BY
RACHEL LEE

MILLS & BOON

Published in Great Britain 2015
by Mills & Boon, an imprint of Harlequin (UK) Limited,
Eton House, 18-24 Paradise Road, Richmond, Surrey, TW9 1SR

© 2015 Susan Civil Brown

ISBN: 978-0-263-25122-7

23-0315

Harlequin (UK) Limited's policy is to use papers that are natural, renewable and recyclable products and made from wood grown in sustainable forests. The logging and manufacturing processes conform to the legal environmental regulations of the country of origin.

Printed and bound in Spain
by CPI, Barcelona

Rachel Lee was hooked on writing by the age of twelve and practiced her craft as she moved from place to place all over the United States. This *New York Times* best-selling author now resides in Florida and has the joy of writing full-time.

To single parents, my admiration.
You have the toughest job in the world.

Chapter One

Hope Conroy sat in the City Diner in Conard City, Wyoming, waiting for a man named Jim Cashford. She had rarely in her life been as nervous as she felt just then.

She needed the job. Her family had cut off her credit cards, she had the last hundred dollars from her bank account in her wallet and she didn't know what in the world she would do if this guy didn't hire her.

Clearly she had not planned her escape well, but her need to get away from Dallas had been urgent. She couldn't take the pressure one more minute.

Instinctively, she lowered her hand to the gentle swell of her belly, a swelling so slight most wouldn't notice it. But she did, just as she felt the little movements that seemed almost like bubbles popping. She would do anything for this baby, except marry the man who had raped her.

She wondered how much she would have to explain

to this Cashford guy. His ad had said he wanted a nanny for a thirteen-year-old daughter. What if he thought a pregnant unwed mother would be a bad example? He'd surely notice soon. It wouldn't be long before the whole world would be able to tell she carried a child.

So somehow she was going to have to explain this. Having a low-paying job for a month or two wasn't going to help her much. A hundred dollars wouldn't buy much gas. She doubted many people would be willing to hire a woman in her state.

When she'd first come in here to get a little something to eat, a newspaper had been sitting on the table. She had snatched it up before the rude woman had demanded to know what she wanted. Skipping immediately to the want ads, the words about the nanny had seemed to leap out at her, and for a few glorious minutes she thought life had delivered her an answer.

But brief as her conversation with Cashford had been, doubts had started to grow immediately. She'd hardly been able to swallow the roll she had ordered and most of it still sat on the plate in front of her. She wondered why he was so quick to come into town to meet with her. Did he have trouble keeping nannies? She feared she might be wasting nearly an hour waiting for him, and that tonight there would be no answer to her problem, merely another cold night sleeping in her car. Then what?

She'd been a fool in so many ways, but even reaching that conclusion didn't show her any other way she could have handled it. She needed care for her child, for one thing, and while she could have gone on assistance in Texas, getting as far as she could from her family's reach had seemed imperative. God, they were like hound dogs with a bone. They wouldn't give up, they wouldn't believe her and they wouldn't let her shame the family. A triad she couldn't escape except with distance.

A dusty pickup pulled up right out front. It must be Cashford. Her mouth turned immediately dry as sand, and her palms moistened. She wondered if her tongue would stick to the roof of her mouth until she sounded like an idiot who couldn't even talk.

A tall, lean, but powerful man climbed out. Despite what Hope considered a chilly day, he didn't wear a jacket. Instead, he had on the basic local uniform of old jeans, cowboy boots, a chambray shirt and a cowboy hat that looked as if it had been a lot of places besides on his head. A working cowboy. She'd seen them some-times in Texas when she got away from the city. Very different from the dudes in Dallas who only wanted to look the part.

Sun and wind had weathered his face some, but she didn't judge him to be terribly old. Maybe forty? A far cry from her twenty-four, but not that huge a leap. Under any other circumstances, she'd have considered him a hunk. Even in the midst of her overwhelming anxiety she felt a prickle of attraction, but quickly quashed it. Never again.

Attractive or not, right now, this guy might be a threat or a savior. She had no idea which.

He walked to the front door with that loose stride shared by people who spent a lot of time in a saddle. He opened it, waving to the grumpy woman who had served her. "Howdy, Maude. How's it going?"

Maude frowned. "Barely getting by, as usual."

"Well, that's good I guess."

Then he turned to scan the small diner with eyes so blue they almost seemed to cast their own light.

"Coffee?" Maude asked him.

"And a slice of your pie." His gaze settled on Hope. "And bring one for the lady here."

Taking off his hat to reveal dark hair that silvered a bit at the temples, he crossed the short distance and thrust his hand out to Hope. She reached up to shake it, finding it warm and work-hardened. "Jim Cashford," he said. "Most folks call me Cash. You're Hope Conroy?"

"Yes."

He smiled. It was a dazzling smile that nearly took her breath away. "Good. I'd hate to be scaring off strange young ladies who weren't looking for me."

He slid into the booth across from her and didn't say anything more until Maude had brought them both huge slices of apple pie with a side of vanilla ice cream. Those plates hit the table with a sharp clatter, but Jim Cashford didn't seem disturbed by it. A mug of coffee followed.

"Want some coffee?" Cashford asked Hope. "Maude makes the best."

"No, thank you. Water is fine."

He forked some pie into his mouth, his blue eyes scanning her. "I'll be up-front," he said when he had swallowed. "I'm not experienced at interviewing for a nanny. I usually interview ranch hands. But my ex died, I've got one unhappy thirteen-year-old, I can't seem to connect with her and I'm working too much. So I want someone closer to her age to be a friend to her as much as anything, but someone old enough to have some sense. You said you studied psychology?"

"Yes, I have. It was my minor."

"You got a driver's license? A reference?"

She felt everything inside her start to crumble. A reference? She hadn't counted on that. With shaking hands, she opened her purse and took out her license.

He studied it. "Dallas?" At that he looked up. "Suppose you tell me what you're doing in the middle of nowhere this far from home?"

There it was. The impossible question. Part of her thought it was time to get up and walk out. But a more desperate part of her took charge. At least she managed to hold back the tears that were trying to make her eyes burn.

Cash waited, studying the young woman in front of him. Pretty enough to knock the wind from a guy. He might not get around much, but there was no mistaking that she was expensively dressed in a well-fitted green slacks suit, perfectly made up, and that her highlighted hair had been maintained by a better hairdresser than any around here. She smelled like money. Was this some kind of game for her?

But there was a pinching around her eyes that told a very different story. This woman had troubles. Aw hell. He was a sucker for a sad story. Maybe he should just finish his pie and head on home.

But then he remembered what would be coming home from school around four o'clock: Angie. His daughter from hell. A teen full of attitude and anger who refused to talk to him unless it was to say something nasty. A hellion. He was sure that somewhere inside he loved his daughter, but that was getting increasingly hard to remember.

So he waited on high alert for whatever tale of woe this woman was selling. What the hey, anyway. She was certainly eye candy, worth a few more minutes of his time with her ash-blond hair and moss-green eyes. Didn't see many like her around here. They tended to get snatched up fast, turned old faster by hard work… or they left on the first bus out.

"You look desperate," he finally said when she seemed unable to speak. Were those tears moistening her eyes? "Look, as long as you're not wanted by the law, I probably won't give a damn."

"I'm not running from the police," she said quietly.

He kind of liked the soft Texas twang in her voice. Just the hint of it, not overpowering. "So tell me what's going on."

She cast her eyes down. "It's very personal."

"Easiest person to tell something personal is a stranger."

"Really?"

"Yeah, you don't have to keep me around like a reminder if you don't want. Get up, walk out, pretend we never talked."

She lifted her gaze, and the faintest smile curved her lips. A little of her anxiety eased. "Are you really that easygoing?"

"I was. I got a daughter who's making me less so. So let me start the truth or dare game. My daughter, Angie, is thirteen. Her mother died four months ago unexpectedly, so now she's living with me. Thing is, she hates me. She can barely stand the sight of me."

"But why?"

"Hell if I know. It's always been that way. But now she's living with me. I'm at wit's end. I spend every minute of my working day worrying that when I get back to the house she'll have run away. She's always spoiling for a fight, too. I need someone to watch her. I hope this someone might get past her granite wall. At this point I don't much care if she ever stops hating me, but I'd be a whole helluva lot happier if I knew someone was keeping her safe. So this isn't going to be an easy job."

She nodded, clearly listening and absorbing. At least she didn't look quite so close to tears.

"So there you have it. An impossible job, an incorrigible kid and a desperate father. You get room and board and lousy pay for the package. Wanna run away now?"

She lifted her hands from her lap, pushed the pie with melting ice cream to the side and folded them together tightly. Slender, delicate fingers, well-manicured. Oh, yeah, he could smell the money. Whatever the outcome, his curiosity became overwhelming.

"Your turn," he said.

She nodded. He tried to wait patiently and filled his mouth with more pie and ice cream to ensure he didn't speak and push her into flight. Even if this came to naught, he wanted to hear the story. It wasn't often anymore that he got to hear a new one. All the stories in these parts had been coming his way for years. An awful lot were reruns just to make conversation.

"I ran away from home," she said finally.

He stiffened. This woman embodied the thing he most feared about Angie. Maybe he should stop right now. But no, she was twenty-four, she'd said, and running away from home at that age raised all kinds of questions.

"What happened?"

"Ugly story." She kept her voice low, and every so often it would crack a little. He leaned in to hear better.

Another long pause, so he ate some more pie.

"Okay," she said. "Short version. My family is prominent in Dallas. The kind of prominence where social connections are important and scandal isn't welcome. I became a scandal."

"You? How's that?"

"Well, they wouldn't believe me. You probably won't,

either. But I was engaged to be married. I thought I loved him. Everybody was thrilled. I'd picked a guy from the right family, if you get me. Everyone's sure he's going to be a senator one day. Except for one little problem."

"You."

"Me."

"But what's wrong with you?"

"Oh, I was raised right, taught all the correct things. You could say I was groomed like a show filly specifically to get to this place."

"But?"

"He raped me."

The words barely emerged from her throat. They sounded so tight that he was sure she almost choked on them.

"To hell with him, then."

"You'd think." She closed her eyes and her hands knotted into fists. "Nobody believed me, of course. Then I found out I was pregnant. I guess that rules me out as a nanny."

For an instant it almost did, but then Cash had another thought. Here was a young woman, pregnant and alone, and a prime example of the dangers in life. She might be a good object lesson. So instead of shutting it all down, he decided to ask more.

"Why'd you have to run away?"

"Because they insisted we push the marriage up and make things all right for Scott. When I swore I'd never marry him, they told me I had to get an abortion. Because if there was one thing that must not happen, it was the kind of scandal that would ruin Scott's future and hurt my family as a result."

"That's medieval!"

"So was the part where they kept me locked up. I didn't get to go anywhere by myself, and then only rarely. It took me months to find a way to escape."

"So you had to either marry your rapist or lose your child?"

"That was it. Oh, and I had to vow never to tell anyone Scott had raped me. Not that anyone believed Scott would do such a thing."

He swore quietly. "Why didn't they just send you to Europe for a year or two? Out of sight and all that?"

"Evidence. There'd always be evidence if I kept this baby. I could threaten him by demanding a paternity test."

"They thought you'd do that?"

"I'd accused him of rape, hadn't I? They were sure I was lying about that. Scott would never do such a thing."

It sounded like a story from another age, or from one of those soap operas his mother had loved so much. Yet looking at Hope across the table, he could see very real pain. She'd have to be a pathological liar to make this up. In fact, a pathological liar probably could have come up with something more believable and inventive.

He sighed. He was going to do this. In his heart of hearts, he knew he couldn't send this woman on her way at least until he knew the truth. He'd have the weekend to see how she interacted with Angie, and he'd make a point of being close by for a while after Angie got home from school.

"I guess," he said, "that there's no one I can call to ask about you?"

"Not even my best friend knows what happened. I'm sorry. I'm wasting your time." Her lower lip quivered.

"I've got an idea. But before we go over to the sheriff's office to check out your license, why don't you eat some of that pie? Looks to me like you need the energy."

He hated treating her suspiciously, but he had a daughter to consider, hellion though she was. The sheriff could find out if she had any warrants or past crimes. Then he was going to hit his computer and see what he could learn about Hope Conroy. If she came from the kind of family she claimed, he'd bet the Dallas newspapers would mention her more than once. And certainly they'd announced this engagement.

Satisfied he wasn't being a total fool, he worked on finishing his pie.

Although Hope knew she had nothing in her background to worry about—as it was, she'd been allowed to do little enough in her life—she still felt nervous walking into the sheriff's office. What if this somehow revealed her whereabouts to her family? And how could she ask about that without having to once again explain her situation?

To her surprise, she and Cash were immediately taken to the sheriff himself in his back office. She guessed that meant her would-be employer had some pull around here.

Cash made the introductions. The sheriff immediately aroused her interest. Gage Dalton moved stiffly as he rose from his chair, wincing faintly, and a burn scar covered one side of his face. She wondered what his story was, but not for long. She was too nervous about all of this to think of much besides herself.

"I'm thinking about hiring Ms. Conroy to help me with Angie," Cash said. "I wondered if we could get a background check."

Gage nodded as he resumed his seat. "Of course." His dark gaze shifted to Hope. "You have ID?"

Here it was. Gathering her courage in her hands, she said, "This won't allow anyone to find me, will it?"

For an instant she thought she'd completely blown it. Her stomach turned over and she felt almost sick enough to vomit.

"Depends," Gage said. "If you have any wants or warrants from law enforcement it will."

"But not my family or friends?"

"Not unless they have an inside line at the DMV or the national criminal database. Is there something I need to know?"

Cash stepped in, saving her. "Ms. Conroy is on the run from a shotgun marriage is all."

"Well, this sure won't help them find you. But you know they can trace you other ways?"

She nodded, her insides now feeling like a leaf shaking in the wind.

"Credit cards, things like that," the sheriff continued. "A good private detective wouldn't take long. Would they send one?"

Now her stomach quit doing somersaults and fell off a cliff. "They might," she admitted.

"We'll cross that bridge if we come to it," Cash said. She darted a glance at him because his voice had turned steely. His jaw looked a bit tight. What had she said?

God, she just wanted to get up right now and run. But she needed this job so badly. She had a child to think of now, and that had to come first. With trembling hands, she once again pulled out her driver's license and turned it over to Gage.

"I can check on this in about ten minutes," Gage said to Cash. "If you want me to go in depth, that might take a couple of days, and Ms. Conroy will have to sign a release."

"Let's just start with this," Cash said. "I can probably find out more of what I need to know online."

Hope looked down at her hands, feeling like a bug under a microscope. But what had she expected? This man was talking about trusting her with his daughter. It wasn't enough to meet over a piece of pie, with her telling a crazy story, and assume everything was copacetic. No way. She understood that.

But she also wasn't used to this. She had come from a world where everyone who mattered knew who she was. She had never had to prove herself in this way. Or in most ways, she realized. Not for the first time in the past few weeks she faced how sheltered she had been. Now all the shelters were gone.

Time to grow up, she thought as they waited for the results of her record to come back. She had a child to think about now, and there was going to be no support from any direction as far as she could tell. Escape meant freedom. Freedom meant responsibility. Simply running wasn't, and would never be, enough.

Ten minutes later, as Gage had promised, a deputy returned her license announcing she was clean, not so much as a parking ticket.

Gage and Cash had been talking generally about people they knew, the local economy and ranching. With a start she realized she hadn't even remotely paid attention.

Not only was that rude, but they must be wondering what was wrong with her. All she knew was that she was tired, frightened, alone and embarking on a task she wasn't sure she could handle.

But then she stiffened herself internally and told herself to stop being a wuss. She'd had three paths out of that situation, and two of them led directly to hell as far as she was concerned. Flight was all that was left to her…and to her child.

Cash rose and shook the sheriff's hand. "Thanks, Gage."

Remembering her manners, Hope summoned a smile and offered her own hand for a shake. "Thank you for your time."

"Good luck to you," Gage said. "Both of you."

Cash laughed, but didn't sound quite happy. "We shall see, I suppose."

Hope guessed they would.

Hope's sporty little silver car looked out of place on the street where she had parked it. It might have had a sign flashing Outsider on it. She couldn't even sell it because it was in her father's name. Entirely too dependent, she thought. Dependent on that man for everything, about to be handed off to a man who had a streak of cruelty she never would have imagined until that night when he took her virginity against her will. A bubble of anger burst in her, but she held it back. Not now. Maybe never. There were more important things than indulging fury about how she had been treated.

Cash had driven her to her car and he climbed out to help her. A gentleman's manners in one who looked like anything but a gentleman. Of course, gentlemen weren't always, were they.

"You won't get to drive that much around here," he said after she climbed in behind the wheel. "You probably won't want to, anyway. It'll take a beating on the roads, especially out toward my place. Speaking of which…"

She looked up, waiting, gripping her keys until they bit into her hand.

"My ranch is pretty isolated. I'm serious. You might go a week or longer without seeing a soul but me, my daughter, my housekeeper and my hired hands. Can you handle that?"

Tension suddenly let go. Isolated. "Right now that sounds wonderful."

"Right now it probably does. Anyway, I've got an old pickup you can use so you won't be stuck out there when Angie's in school. You can run on into town if you need to. But most of the time—" he shrugged "—I hope you like horses and cows."

"I love horses. I haven't been close to too many cows."

"Now's your chance. Well, if you're not changing your mind, follow me. We should get home a little before Angie gets off the bus, so you'll have a chance to settle in and look around."

"Thank you. Sincerely."

His eyes crinkled in the corners. "Tell me that again after you've met my daughter."

That almost sounded like a threat, Hope thought as she turned on her car and pulled out to follow his truck. Then her mood shifted abruptly. It had been doing that a lot lately, but all of a sudden she felt almost giddy. Relief for starters. She had a job.

A bubble of laughter escaped her, and a genuine smile softened her face for the first time in months. And for the first time, she actually noticed that it was a pretty September day.

Leading the way, Cash wondered if he'd lost his marbles. On the other hand, asking this woman to be a companion to Angie seemed better than having Angie racketing about all by herself too much of the time. All that seemed to do was heighten her hostility.

But if her anger with him had a dial to turn it down a notch or two, he hadn't found it.

He was, he admitted, totally at a loss. When Sandy had left him, Angie had still been in diapers. In one fell swoop, he'd lost wife and daughter to distance. He couldn't make as many visits as he might have liked because of the demands of work, and Sandy had moved all the way to Arizona. He still felt guilty about that, but over the years as Angie had distanced him, even during his visits, the guilt had become easier to live with. Now she was in his house and broken connections, or at least damaged ones, stared him in the face.

He quite simply didn't know how to reach her.

Which brought him to this moment in time. Leading a strange woman, a pregnant runaway, home in the hopes that she might be able to at least keep the girl safer. That maybe she could reach Angie at least a bit.

That she could somehow find a way around all his screwups as a father. Because he really did hold himself responsible for this. Clearly he'd failed in some essential way, and blaming it on distance didn't excuse him. He wondered if he was missing some basic instinct or knowledge. Wondered what he could have done differently, how he could have changed things. No answers arrived.

He reminded himself that his daughter was still grieving her mother. That was killer all by itself. But in the meantime, he had to do something. He couldn't just leave her alone for long stretches of time to brood and hurt and fuel her anger. She needed someone, and he was working long hours. The ranch demanded almost all he had in these hard times and didn't leave a whole lot of room for so-called bonding experiences. Not that Angie would let him get that close.

His life had turned into a snarled mess. He wasn't blaming his daughter for it, but she was a problem he couldn't evade. He had to help her somehow.

Hence a young woman from Dallas. He just hoped he hadn't misjudged Hope Conroy, because she was the first person to answer his ad who wasn't even older than he was. He felt he needed someone closer to Angie in age, someone who might actually be able to be her friend instead of her guard.

Although Angie probably wouldn't note the difference. He could hear what was coming already.

The ranch was beautiful, Hope thought. As they at last turned into what she supposed must be his driveway, she took in the wide-open space with its backdrop of high mountains. They were turning purple as the afternoon sun sank toward them.

There weren't a whole lot of cattle in sight but she still saw clusters of them scattered like a natural blessing in the open fields. They looked fat and happy.

The house itself rose two stories amid a stand of tall trees. White clapboard gleamed in the sunlight and a wide porch covered the entire front side. Wooden chairs dotted the porch and to one side hung a wooden bench swing.

Inviting. More inviting than the perfect showplace in which she had grown up with its manicured lawns and tall pillars, as if it were trying to imitate an antebellum plantation.

This house looked as if it belonged, and apart from it, the fences provided the only sign that man was here.

She pulled up on the gravel beside Cash's truck and

climbed out. No sound greeted her except the soft sigh of the breeze. It was chillier here than at home, but she found it invigorating.

Cash approached her. "Welcome," he said. "Let's go inside and get you settled. You have bags, I presume?"

"I'll get them."

"I'll help."

Hope opened her trunk, revealing her set of matched Louis Vuitton bags. She thought she saw his eyebrows lift, but it was hard to be sure under that battered cowboy hat.

She'd never thought about that luggage before, but she thought about it now. Those bags shrieked status and money as they were intended to do. She actually felt embarrassed by them. Boy, her worldview was undergoing some radical shifts.

She followed him willingly up the steps, across the porch and in through the front door. She tugged her rolling carry-on and hung her personal care bag over her shoulder. Cash hefted the two larger ones as if they weighed nothing at all.

Inside she was surprised by a large foyer with heavily polished wood floors and a wide wood staircase leading upstairs. Clearly this ranch had known some good times. Either that or someone was very much into carpentry. He led her up the stairs.

"My housekeeper comes three times a week so I'm not asking you to clean or cook."

Hope was glad to hear it because she'd never seriously cleaned or cooked in her life. Yeah, she'd done bits of both, especially when she wanted to try out her baking skills in high school, but mostly all of that had been taken care of. Something else she was going to need to learn. She wondered if the housekeeper would help her.

At the top of the stairs, they turned right and he showed her into a spacious but simply furnished room. There was a bed, a rocking chair, a bureau with mirror. Small rugs scattered the floor with color, while everything else was fairly plain, even the curtains.

"This is yours," he said, putting her bags down. "Take your time. The bathroom is that way down the hall, and Angie is right across from you. I'm at the other end."

He glanced at his watch. "She'll be home in an hour."

"I'll be ready."

"She won't be." Then he flashed a crooked smile and vanished, closing the door behind him.

She sank onto the edge of the bed, looking around herself, thinking about how rapidly life could change. The rape, her escape and flight, and now her first real job. Until this moment, the majority of her thoughts had been focused on getting away and trying not to think about the horror Scott had inflicted on her. Now, in a strange room in a strange place, she realized her challenges had only just begun.

Relief at having this chance to prove herself gave way to determination to succeed. Somehow, some way, she was going to do this job right.

In the meantime, she decided to scrub the makeup from her face, put her hair in a ponytail and don one of her few pairs of jeans. The rest of her clothes would be useless here, utterly out of place. Regardless, pretty soon nothing would fit. It was getting hard to button her jeans. She'd have to do something about that.

It was time to make the rest of her transformation.

Downstairs, Cash went into his office and started his computer. He closed his financial files and began to search the internet for Hope. If any of her story was true, he'd find the important pieces here.

It didn't take him long. Hope Conroy was a well-known name in the Dallas newspaper. Her engagement photo with a handsome man only a few years older than she was blazed across nearly the entire top of one page. Beneath was a detailed and saccharine description of her, her fiancé—definitely touted as a man with a bright future in politics—and their families. In one swoop he picked up enough information to get a pretty clear picture that she wasn't exaggerating about scandal. These folks wouldn't put up with it.

She was mentioned surprisingly often, appearing at charity balls, participating in various volunteer activities, none of which had much to do with the underside of life except for one large homeless charity where she sat on a board.

There was more, raising his eyebrows with each revelation. Money, more money than he could imagine, colored every word. He knew girls who wanted to be barrel riders, not girls who participated in dressage. But Hope had, for a while.

He nearly put his head in his hands when he finished reading.

He had hired a twenty-four-carat, hot damn, for real Texas princess.

Chapter Two

Just about the time the school bus would drop Angie at the end of the driveway, Cash emerged from his office. He discovered Hope standing nervously in the foyer, dressed in clothes that looked better in these parts even if the designer label on her jeans didn't. No makeup, which to his way of thinking made her prettier, and the ponytail at least softened the too-perfect hair.

A damned Texas princess. The thought was still rolling around in his head, and he was wrestling with the possibility that he had just made a big mistake. He'd picked up that she'd come from money, he just hadn't guessed what kind of money. If she started filling Angie's head with stories of trips to ski in the Alps and parties on private yachts, he didn't know what he was going to do. His daughter already owned enough discontent to fill half the Pacific Ocean.

Unfortunately for Angie, she was a rancher's daughter, not the daughter of a billionaire. She had to make peace with that somehow, at least until she could leave for college. Of course, it would be a state college, not some place like Radcliffe or Vassar, but it would give her a leg up if she didn't want to stay here. He suspected she wouldn't, and that was okay. But he had to keep her expectations and dreams on enough of a leash to at least get through high school in one piece.

He seriously doubted that Hope would be the one to do it.

As she turned to him, he spoke without preamble. "Angie's going to walk through that door any minute. So I want something clear."

She questioned him with a look from moss-green eyes.

"I read up about you in the papers. Not many people enjoy the advantages you had, and my kid never will. I don't want you filling her head with fairy-tale dreams she can never have."

"Fairy tales don't always have happy endings," she said. "Trust me, the less I talk about my past, the better. All those advantages? They turned into a prison and they're gone now. At this point in time, your daughter has a brighter future than I do."

He liked the spark he saw in her then, a brief flash of anger, and a whole lot of clear-eyed determination. "Okay, then."

"I've got a lot to learn," Hope said after a moment. "Maybe Angie and I can learn together."

He wondered what she meant by that, but before he could answer, the door flew open and Angie stormed in. A dark-haired girl, she wore jeans and a sweatshirt emblazoned with the name of a band. She hadn't even got inside and she was already looking for a fight. Fire filled her dark eyes, and she slung her book bag onto the floor. It slid until it hit the wall.

"That school sucks," she announced before anyone could greet her. "Some of the boys smell like cows and manure. The teachers are stupid. The whole place is stupid." Then her flashing eyes landed on Hope. "What's this? Your girlfriend? Or my keeper? Either way, I don't want her here." She glared at Hope. "Get out of here. Now."

Then she ran up the stairs, leaving her bag where it had fallen, punctuating her rant by slamming the door upstairs hard enough to make the windows rattle a bit.

The sound of the girl stomping around in her room overhead became all that filled the silence.

Hope cleared her throat. "She's very pretty."

"Pretty is as pretty does," Cash remarked. "There you have it. If she has any other mode of communication, I haven't seen it. Still want to take this on?"

"I want to try," Hope answered without hesitation. She gave him a wan smile. "I understand anger. I've been living with enough of it for several months now. She just lost her mother, you said. Well, I lost my innocence, so maybe we're not very different."

"You're handling it a lot better."

"Only because I'm older and well trained. One mustn't make a scene, you know. Not that I think Angie shouldn't be permitted to express herself. God knows, bottling it up does no good." She sighed. "Show me around? I need to know where things are and what your rules are."

"I don't have a whole lot of rules," he said, waving her toward the kitchen. "I'd like some courtesy in communications, but basically, as long as it isn't dangerous, no rules. There are always snacks for her, Hattie, my housekeeper makes sure there are fresh cookies in the jar. I'd like Angie to get her homework done every day, but trying to police that only results in another scene like the one you just saw."

"Do you have any reason to think she isn't getting it done?"

"I asked the teachers to let me know."

"Then I guess it's safe to assume she is. What else? Especially the dangerous part."

"No taking a horse out alone. She's welcome to ride, but not alone. That infuriates her because she has to wait for one of my hands or me, and she'd rather die than go with me."

"Well, I can ride with her if she wants. More?"

"If she rides, she has to take care of her mount afterward. We've been having a problem with that."

For the first time, Hope looked honestly astonished. "Really? I took care of my horses. Part of the drill. Okay, I'll make it clear, if she's willing to ride with me."

He paused as they stood in the kitchen. "I'm not a hard man, Hope. But this is my first experience of raising a child and I'm sure I'm fumbling. I don't want to saddle her with limitations and rules, but she needs to pick up after herself, leave the bathroom usable by another person, and do her own laundry. I don't have maid service."

He thought Hope flushed faintly. "Did she have it before?"

"No, and that's what makes this so strange."

"More of her resentment," Hope suggested. "It's got to be hard to lose your mother. What happened, if I'm not being too nosy?"

"Peritonitis. Fast and hard, from what I understand, but I don't have all the details. By the time Sandy felt sick enough to go to the hospital, it was too late. A matter of hours."

Hope nodded and looked down. "She must have been terrified. Angie, I mean. To have that happen so fast, and it's not even like a car accident. Her mom was sick—they should have been able to help her."

"I hadn't thought of that." Cash contemplated that for a minute, realizing that he probably hadn't spent enough time thinking of what his daughter was dealing with. He'd been too busy dealing with her. Ah, damn, another failure on his part.

He looked at Hope. "I know I'm asking a lot, but try to be a friend to her. Before you, I had two very grand-motherly ladies apply for the job. This time I wanted someone closer to her age. Someone she could feel closer to, if that's possible."

Hope nodded slowly. "I'd guess that right now the last thing she would want would be someone trying to stand in for her mother."

"Hell, she doesn't even want a father. But I get what you're saying. I'm not expecting miracles, though I'd like to see her a little happier and a little more comfort-able here. I'm not totally oblivious. She didn't just lose her mother—she lost her home, her friends, her school. The school counselor is trying to work with her, but so far she's just not talking. Well, except to yell at me."

"I'm sure this is hard on you."

"I'm not looking for sympathy," he said frankly. "I don't need it. That girl needs something, and clearly I'm not giving it to her."

"I'll try," Hope said. "That's all I can do."

"It's all I can ask."

Cash excused himself, saying he needed to get back to work. The stomping from upstairs had ceased, and Hope could only guess what Angie might be doing.

Sleeping? Crying? Or just fuming? Anything was possible, especially since she didn't know the girl at all.

She hesitated, then decided to make a cup of tea and settle in for a while, awaiting the next development. The tea bags sat on the counter next to an electric kettle and a coffeemaker brimming with what smelled like fresh brew. At least she knew how to make tea, from her years at college. Beyond that, a kitchen was mostly alien territory to her, although she supposed she could have managed coffee. As a child she'd spent some time with her family's cook in the kitchen, watching and messing with dough, but cooking a whole meal? No way.

Nor would she ever have needed to learn if she had continued her directed path in life. Scott could have kept her in the same style she'd been raised to. She'd have spent her future on the boards of various charities, raising a child or two with the help of nannies, making public appearances for Scott when he wanted her to. A smooth and seamless transition from one life of privilege to the next.

But it hadn't turned out that way. Part of her was still reeling from the rape, but she had managed to lock that away in a tight box because she had more important things to worry about, like escaping that man and saving her baby.

Perhaps the biggest shock of all, aside from the rape, had been her own family's unwillingness to believe her. She was their daughter; surely they knew she wouldn't invent such a lie? How could the change in her have been so invisible to them—one day the happy fiancée of a man who was going places, the next absolutely determined to ditch Scott? Didn't that mean anything to them?

Could people be so willfully blind?

Apparently so. Sighing, she sat with her tea at the wooden kitchen table. She didn't feel comfortable enough yet to explore the house on her own. One didn't do that in someone else's house, even if they were now an employee.

Or did being an employee make it even more out of line? How would she know? God, she had a lot to learn.

She heard footsteps on the stairs and tensed, wondering if she was about to be faced with another ragefest, or if Angie would simply slip out the door. If she left, was Hope supposed to follow her? Apart from the matters she didn't know about caring for herself, there were a lot of big blanks in this job description. Try to be a friend to the girl? That would depend on Angie.

But the steps crossed the foyer, and Angie was entering the kitchen. Hope hesitated, then said, "Hi."

The girl didn't answer. She headed straight for the coffeepot and filled a mug, topping it with cream.

Hope waited, half expecting the girl to disappear again. But she didn't. Instead, she came over to the big table, put her mug down with an audible bang and yanked out a chair to sit. Clearly she wasn't over her anger.

"So who are you and what are you doing here?" Angie demanded.

"My name is Hope. Your dad hired me because he's concerned about you being alone so much."

"If he cared, he'd spend more time at home."

Hope didn't respond to that. Angie still wasn't looking at her, and her long dark hair concealed most of her face.

"I don't need a babysitter," Angie snapped.

"I don't think you do."

"Yeah?" The girl looked at her, her eyes snapping with anger. "Then what good are you?"

Good question, thought Hope. "I guess that's for you to decide. Your dad said he didn't have many rules so it seems it's up to you and me to work out something."

"That sounds like him. Let someone else figure it out. Well, you can go, because as far as I'm concerned, I don't need you."

"But I need this job, at least for a while," Hope said honestly. "I'd appreciate it if you'd help me out."

Some infinitesimal shift took place in Angie's expression. She didn't appear to soften, but something changed. Hope tensed, wondering if she'd just made a huge mistake. Basically she'd given this child power over her, and if there was one thing she had learned, it was how the strands of power flowed.

"Where are you from?" Angie asked after a few seconds. "Not from around here. Your accent."

"Texas."

"You came a long way for a crappy job."

"So it appears."

"But you didn't come all this way for this job."

Obviously not, Hope thought, but how much did she want to say. She'd already been through her personal wringer explaining to Cash, and besides, this girl was young. She didn't need the ugly details. "No," she finally answered cautiously.

"Something wrong at home?"

That put Hope squarely on the horns of a dilemma. If she said yes, she was running away, Angie might get her own ideas about running. She picked her words carefully. "There's a guy. He wouldn't leave me alone."

"Not a nice guy?"

"Definitely not."

Angie nodded slowly. "My mom had a problem with one of those. She got a restraining order, but she was still frightened. For a while she wouldn't even allow me to walk to school by myself."

"That must have been scary for you."

"Sort of." Angie guzzled some coffee with little finesse. "Did you grow up on a ranch?"

"No."

"Well, it's the most boring place on earth. Take it from me. In a couple of weeks you'll be begging to get out of here. There's nothing to do, everybody works all the time and I'm not even allowed to ride a horse unless someone comes with me. Since nobody has time, I just sit here and watch the clock."

"No friends yet to talk with?"

"No." Angie's face darkened.

"Well, I can't do anything about that. But I *can* take you riding."

For the briefest instant, Angie's face brightened. Then the dour look returned. "We'll see," she said darkly. Then she refilled her mug and left the kitchen, clomping her way up the stairs.

Angie had revealed a lot, yet very little. Hope had plenty to think about as she finished her tea then stepped outside to take a brief stroll.

The rapid cooling of the afternoon surprised her. It hadn't been that long since she arrived, but the sun was sinking behind the mountains now, and the air held a definite nip. She ignored it instead of getting her jacket and just walked around the house, taking in the setting and the expanses.

She could understand why Hope was bored here. No friends to spend hours on the phone with, no place to go, unable to ride without an escort. Yet at the same time there were beauties here that cried out for exploration. Some of the cattle had come close to the fence out back, and she walked over to them, ignoring the chill that was beginning to make her shiver.

One with big, dark brown eyes paid attention to her. Clearly a female, she watched Hope's approach placidly enough, yet alertly. Hope reached the fence and stood still, waiting to see what would happen.

The breeze stiffened and bit into her back and neck. She wasn't going to be able to stand here for long, but the cow interested her. Step by step, the bovine came closer. Hope wondered if she was expecting some kind of treat or was just curious. She couldn't imagine what a cow would want as a treat.

Horses liked apples and carrots and sugar cubes, but a cow? She could have laughed at her own ignorance. How many cattle barons did she know? Quite a few, actually. Men who had made it and could spend a lot of time in the city while others worked their ranches.

Not like Cash. Her thoughts drifted back to him and what he had said about working so much of the time. Not one of the lucky barons, evidently. But then nothing about him suggested the softness of wealth and being able to rely on others to do a job. She would have bet he could do any job on this ranch himself, and probably often did.

She heard the crunching of dried grass behind her and turned to see Cash walking toward her. In the almost eerie light of a world still bright with the sun in hiding behind the mountains, she thought he looked part and parcel of this ranch of his.

"How's it going and where's your jacket?" He'd donned a denim one with lining.

"I just stepped out for a minute."

"Clearly Texas girls don't know how fast it gets cold here in the afternoon. Are you communing with my cows?"

She looked back at the big black one that had been watching her. "I'm not sure. She's been moving slowly closer, like she's curious."

"She probably is. Cattle have more brains than most folks credit them. Did you see Angie again?"

"We talked briefly."

"And?"

"There might be a chance for rapport. It's too soon to tell."

He flashed a small smile. "I'll take that as a good sign. Come on, you need to get inside. I can see you're shivering."

For the first time she realized she was. Wrapping her arms around herself, she walked with him toward the back of the house. "So do you give cows treats like horses?"

"Some fresh alfalfa or corn makes 'em happy. But no sugar and stuff like that." He gave a piercing whistle without warning and Hope's ears winced.

"What was that?" she asked.

"Calling the dogs. It's feeding time."

For an instant, she was almost overwhelmed as six dogs came racing from every direction, tongues lolling, feet pounding the ground. From behind her, a cow mooed loudly. For just an instant, she felt a flash of fear. What if they bit her?

But then Cash gave another whistle and they fell in behind him like a troop of orderly soldiers.

"They're well behaved," she couldn't help saying.

"They're working dogs. No nonsense. But yes, you can pet them."

At that a laugh escaped her. She felt so good right

now that she wished this moment would never end. She was in a new place with so much to learn, with a challenging girl to deal with and a job.

And with Cash. Astonished, she almost missed a step. After Scott, she had thought she would never again feel attracted to any man. They couldn't be trusted. But something about this man said differently.

She hoped she wasn't developing delusions. And to save herself from that train of thought, she hopped to another track. "I think Angie would like me to take her riding."

"Be my guest. I've got some good mounts in the barn, one gentle enough for her. One challenging enough for you, among others."

"What makes you think I need a challenge?" She looked up at him and found him smiling beneath the brim of his hat.

"Background research. Dressage, huh?"

"Well, yes, but that was a while ago, and I'm pregnant now. How about you suggest a mare so old and gentle she wouldn't think about bucking me off."

He was still chuckling when they reached the house and he began filling a row of stainless-steel bowls with kibble for the dogs. Nearby was a huge tub of water.

"Can they come inside?" she asked.

"Sometimes. Generally I wait until they're getting old and creaky before I make a habit of it. I figure they're entitled to lie by a warm fire when they retire. Most of these guys are pretty young, though."

"Don't want to spoil them?"

"I don't think I could. They love working. But they're also dusty, dirty and full of grass and other things. Not exactly fit for the house."

"Do you groom them?"

He laughed. "Of course. Much good it does, though. But yeah, I don't leave them covered with burrs, ticks or fleas. I take good care of 'em, I just can't keep them clean unless I keep them inside, and that's not going to happen. Unless you've seen a dog flop on your couch and a cloud of dust arise from its coat, you can't imagine."

She supposed she couldn't. The only dogs in her life had been her mother's cherished Yorkies, who never went outside, and the dogs at the horse stables.

Inside, he announced that he was going up to shower. Before he vanished, however, he pulled three serving-size glass dishes from the freezer and popped them in the oven.

"Lasagna for dinner in about an hour," he said, then headed upstairs.

Left at loose ends again, Hope helped herself to more tea. When she turned from the counter, mug in hand, she was startled to see Angie, who looked angry. The girl's tone was sharp.

"You're spying on me for him!"

Startled, all Hope could answer was, "No."

"Yes, you are. I saw you out there talking to him. What did you do? Tell him everything I said to you?"

"The only thing I said about you was that you and I wanted to go riding." Hope felt a spark of anger of her own. "He said he'd show me the horses in the morning so we could. Then we talked about the dogs. Am I going to have to report on every conversation we have to you? Because if so, life isn't going to be pleasant for either of us. I don't spy on anyone."

With that, tea in hand, she marched past Angie and went to sit in the living room. Almost as soon as her bottom met the seat, she regretted her anger. This was not a good start.

But to her surprise, Angie followed her a minute later. "Those are designer jeans," she said. "You don't belong here."

"We'll see."

"Are you some kind of rich bitch?"

The word shocked Hope and she hoped she managed to hide her reaction. This girl was trying to push her buttons, and she couldn't allow it or she'd be done here in a few days. "Not anymore," she said flatly.

"What happened?"

"Maybe I'll tell you someday, when I learn I can trust you."

Hope thought she glimpsed a tiny bit of uncertainty behind Angie's angry expression, but it vanished quickly. She received another angry glare, then listened as the girl pounded back up the stairs to her bedroom.

This was not going well. She felt a wave of near-despair along with drowning fatigue. She reminded herself not to expect much. After all, she'd only been here a few hours. And the fatigue itself was to be expected. Not Angie's fault, but the fault of a long, stress-filled day.

Resting her hand over her stomach, she allowed her eyes to close. A little nap might help, she thought, letting her head fall backward against the sofa. She'd get through this somehow because she had to. There was absolutely no other option. Not yet.

Scott's face swam before her eyes, filling her with a rush of adrenaline and fury. No. Not him. He was gone for good. Don't think about him.

At last exhaustion released her.

When she awoke, she had a crick in her neck. She twisted it immediately, trying to ease it, then saw the room was dimly lit by a single lamp. Opening her eyes wider, she found Cash at the other end of the room in a green plaid-covered armchair, reading a magazine. He appeared absorbed. Several matching armchairs dotted the room, looking weary and worn. The sofa on which she had dozed was also green, but plain and a bit lumpy. No Angie in sight. She knew a moment's shame at how much relief she felt. That girl was a handful, and she could only feel sympathy for her father. She understood that Angie had been through a terrible experience, but she seemed determined to push everyone away.

When she shifted some more, Cash looked up from his magazine. "Hungry? Your lasagna is still warm in the oven."

"Thanks. I'll get it."

"Nah. It's no problem. I'll bring it out here and put it on a TV tray. You like salad? We've got tossed greens and some Caesar dressing."

"That sounds wonderful." Her mouth started watering before she even got all the sleep out of her eyes. For the first time she realized she had eaten very little that day. A hearty meal would probably make her feel a whole lot better about everything.

She felt marginally more awake by the time Cash returned with her meal and a beverage. "Thank you so much, but you really don't need to wait on me."

"You just woke up. It's okay."

Then he returned to his chair and resumed reading while she ate. As famished as she suddenly realized she was, she was glad he didn't try to converse or keep her company. What looked like a large serving of lasagna disappeared rapidly, along with the salad. By the time she finished, she felt more than full, yet it wasn't long before her spirits and energy began reviving.

"I needed that," she remarked.

He looked up and smiled. "I saw how little you ate all day. You didn't even finish Maude's pie. I guess I'll hear about that next time I'm in."

"Did I insult her?"

"Probably, but it's easy to insult Maude. She'll get over it as long as you don't make a practice of it."

"I doubt I'll go there very often." She needed to save every penny from this job. She lifted the table, moving it back, and started to reach for her dishes.

"I'll help."

She glanced at Cash and caught her breath. She recognized a look of pure male appreciation when she saw it. She'd seen it often enough. Instead of feeling flattered, however, this time she felt as if little ice crystals grew inside her. Never again. No man would ever have his way with her again. As far as she was concerned, it was just fine if no man ever touched her again. Touches were lies and then they could be followed by demands that turned violent. As with Scott, who simply refused to accept her decision to wait for their marriage. The ugly names he had called her remained branded on her heart, and the memory of his greater strength, the way he had subdued her against her wishes and then violated her… No, never again.

"Did I say something wrong?"

She came back to the present with a start. Cash now stood only a few feet away, his hand extended as if about to lift her plate. "No…no. Just a…memory."

"Not a good one." But he didn't pursue it. Instead, he helped with the dishes, showing her the dishwasher and then giving her a five-cent tour of the kitchen so she could find anything she was likely to need.

As soon as he finished, though, she pled fatigue. "I'm

really tired. Do you mind if I go up now? Once I catch up on some sleep, I'll be fine."

He nodded, his eyes narrowing a bit. As she started to walk out toward the stairs, his voice stopped her. "Have you seen a doctor? About the baby, I mean?"

She froze, her back to him. "Not yet."

"I think it's high time. Don't tell me you can't afford it. I'll see to it."

She kept walking, unsure whether she felt annoyed by his presumption or simply glad that someone cared enough to help. She'd needed to see a doctor for months now, but it hadn't been allowed. Her family didn't want this baby unless she married Scott, and if she went to any doctor it would be for a discreet abortion. To see a local obstetrician might set tongues wagging.

She'd tried to escape long enough to see a doctor. She hadn't managed, not with all the eyes ordered to watch her every minute. She couldn't get out the door without a keeper.

Hand over her stomach, she mounted the stairs, still astonished by the rabbit hole one man had shoved her into. No proper prenatal care. No one to believe her story except a stranger in Wyoming. Her entire family had turned on her and had treated her worse than they would have treated a prized racehorse that might be off the circuit because she had come unexpectedly into foal.

Oh, she didn't miss the parallels. From birth she had been groomed for one thing. Maybe the saddest thing of all was that she had been naive enough to believe they loved her. Instead, brutally, she had learned that she was simply a chip on the poker table of life.

Cash had been right. The whole thing had been medieval.

When she entered her room and closed the door,

ready to sink onto a soft bed with a book, she froze. Even though she'd been in here only briefly today, she felt something had changed.

Looking around, she couldn't imagine why she felt that way. Did the air smell different? How would she know, as little time as she'd spent in here?

She turned on all the lights, looking more closely, then saw that the closet door stood open just a tiny bit. At once she went over and opened it. One look told her everything. Her suitcases were not as she had left them. Someone had been looking through her luggage.

Angie.

She sat on the edge of the bed and stared into the closet, wondering how to handle this. Most of the cases were locked, and unless the girl was a wizard who could guess combinations, she probably hadn't been able to get into them.

An almost laugh escaped her when she thought of how that must have frustrated the girl. But the issue was bigger than that and she knew it. Angie had no business trying to get into her bags. It was an invasion of privacy, supremely rude and possibly indicated an intent to steal something. She decided, however, that unless there was some other action on Angie's part, she should just ignore it. Making an accusation might only ruin any possibility of getting through to her.

Standing, she unfastened her jeans and sighed with relief as they loosened, but this time she didn't think about how much she needed to get some maternity clothes. Her mind was firmly fixed on Angie, and she lay back on the bed, staring at the ceiling, looking for any key to the lock around Angie's heart.

She didn't know the girl well yet, but she'd picked up on a few things. Maybe riding with her tomorrow would help loosen the steel bands Angie insisted on wrapping around herself. Or maybe not.

The truth was, Hope felt even more at sea now than she had this morning. More unanswered questions faced her than before.

But she made up her mind that she wasn't going to give up on Angie, no matter how hard it was.

Because, frankly, she could see herself in that young woman. The self that was angry, bitter, hurting, betrayed and all the rest of it. She just didn't make a show of it.

Angie was crying out for help in all the wrong ways. Maybe.

Downstairs, Cash poured himself a bourbon and carried it into his office. He sat staring at the darkened computer screen, knowing he should take care of some business, but his mind was unwilling. He had too much else to think about.

There was Angie, of course. There was always Angie. His daughter was a puzzle within a puzzle, and he couldn't see the first chink or move to make. His repertoire of fatherly actions was limited, no question. He had no real experience to guide him, and the years lost between them weren't helping.

But he'd been struck by Hope's comment about Angie being angry because her mother should have been saved. He hadn't considered that before at all. To him, the loss of life for someone so young was the same, no matter the means. But Hope had cast it in a different light, and he would have bet that she was right. Sick people were supposed to get well unless it was something like cancer, and how much more true that must seem for someone Angie's age. The idea that an infection could kill someone so swiftly must be beyond her ability to believe.

Then there was Hope herself, who had until recently led a charmed life it seemed. Now she was cast alone, friendless and penniless on the waters of a world she knew nothing about. When he thought about the fact that she hadn't yet seen a doctor about her pregnancy, anger burned in the pit of his stomach. He simply couldn't imagine people who thought the way her family evidently did. No care for the child, no real care for Hope, who was their daughter. More concern for a guy who might be a senator one day, a guy who wasn't even family.

Twisted. Very twisted.

He rolled the glass slowly between his hands, warming the bourbon and thinking about his newest employee. Maybe she would work out, maybe she wouldn't. He certainly wouldn't hold her accountable if she couldn't get through to Angie. Hell, he'd been trying for months now.

But he could ensure she had a place to stay until this baby came, and that she received decent care. That seemed the least he could do.

She was an awfully attractive woman. It was hard to look at her without noticing her appeal. Given her past, though, he put a big mental off-limits sign on her. No way could life on a ranch hold her long-term, and more importantly, she'd been raped. It'd be a long time before she'd be inclined to see men as anything but a threat. Couldn't blame her for that.

Although he had to give her credit for the way she had handled this day. She'd accepted a job from a strange man and had come home with him. She must be desperate beyond belief to cross those hurdles as bravely as she had. "Single father" in that ad should have been enough to make her skip even calling.

The fact that she had gathered her courage to call him told him plenty. Hope Conroy was at the end of her rope to the point that she was willing to take a huge risk.

Desperate enough that maybe she hadn't even evaluated the risks he might pose. More frightened for herself and her baby than anything else.

Understanding drove through him like a spike. He supposed that made her tougher than a lot of people. Surprising, given her life until recently. Or maybe he didn't really understand that, either. Regardless, she had a lot of backbone. Or maybe she was past thinking clearly about some things.

Either way, a decent man owed her some protection. That much he could do.

Tomorrow was another day, he reminded himself, sipping his whiskey. He needed to wrap up a few things before they got out of hand, then head up to bed. It was the time of year when 5 a.m. seemed to come awfully early.

Chapter Three

In the morning Hope awoke with a considerably clearer head and a much calmer state of being. She'd managed to hold off the wolf at the door, at least temporarily. She had a roof and room and board for as long as she could manage to hang on to them.

It only struck her as she sat up and peeked out to see it was still dark what a huge risk she had taken yesterday. Not in applying for a job, but in coming home with a man she knew nothing about, except that he seemed to get along well with a sheriff she didn't know, either. Given what Scott had done to her, given that she had known him for years and he'd still turned into a monster, she wondered where her brain had been.

But as she felt the very faint stirring of the child within her, she knew. She'd given up everything to save this child without entering into a marriage that could only be hell. One thing and only one thing drove her.

She needed to keep that in mind now when she made decisions, because the one she had made yesterday could
have turned out badly for both her and her baby.

At the time she had seen no other choice. Frankly,
standing at the window staring into darkness, she admitted she had had no other choice except to push on
as far as she could with her remaining cash and hope
she didn't wind up stranded in the middle of nowhere.
She'd been heading toward mountains with no idea if
she could make it across, if she would freeze to death
sleeping in her car, if…

But enough. She stopped herself. She had been
caught between the devil and the deep blue sea, and
she had chosen to jump. So far so good. So far she was
lucky. Just lucky.

Perhaps, through sheer chance, she had managed to
land on her feet. Hanging on to that hopeful thought,
she dressed for the day in a simple sweater and the same
snug jeans. Clothes were going to turn into a problem,
she thought again. She'd packed everything she had
thought she would need, but she hadn't packed for this
lifestyle. Of course, it wasn't as if she had a closet full
of clothes meant for a ranch. At least she had brought
her riding boots, although she wasn't sure why. A me-
mento from a happier time? Maybe. She tugged them
on and pulled the jeans down over them. Riding boots
were not the same as cowboy boots, and she didn't want
to draw too much attention to them. Even if Cash said
nothing, Angie would.

Angie. Her luggage. She wondered again if she should
address that, then once again decided to wait and see.
She was definitely sure that she shouldn't tell Cash about
it, though. That would create entirely the wrong impression with Angie, one that might never be corrected.

Downstairs she found Cash puttering around making eggs and bacon. Her mouth watered immediately. He glanced up from the stove with a smile. "I heard you moving so I made extra. I hope you're hungry."

"Starving."

"Good. Grab some coffee if you want, then grab a seat. You past the morning sickness?"

"I never had it really bad and it seems to be gone."

"Or you'd be running from the smell of the bacon," he said humorously.

"Too true."

"So how far along are you?"

"Approaching four months."

He paused in the process of turning bacon. "Four months? Good God, wouldn't they let you have any care at all? Can they still force you to have an abortion this late?"

"They wouldn't let me anywhere near a doctor unless I agreed to an abortion." She hesitated, her heart sickening. "There's still time. It wouldn't matter, anyway. Money buys nearly everything, even doctors who will discreetly ignore the law."

He finished flipping the bacon, then leaned back to look at her, his arms folded. "I'm sorry. I realize it's none of my business, but I just can't get the thinking behind this. It's like your ex-fiancé is more important than you. Than their own grandchild."

"The baby was a problem unless we got married right away. Then I became a problem when I refused to marry Scott and threatened to pitch a public fit if they dragged me to a wedding in front of a judge or notary."

"I still don't get it."

"I don't get it, either. I certainly wasn't expecting

this. I thought when I told them what Scott had done, they'd be on my side."

"This can't all just be about scandal. Even a scandal that might keep Scott from the senate."

"You wouldn't think. But scandal was all I heard about, that and how I wasn't going to ruin a young man's promising future with my selfishness. It really got ugly. So here I am. The explanations are theirs not mine."

"Do you have any?"

"Considering how all this blindsided me? No."

He went back to making the bacon and started popping toast into a toaster. "Well, whatever is behind it, you know how you were treated. You said you were under house arrest. How the hell did you get away with more than the clothes on your back?"

"I said I was going to see my Great-Aunt Mary in Austin. I claimed I needed time to think, and they knew she agreed with them. They even made arrangements with her so I'd be properly watched. They thought I was flying and arranged for me to be escorted to my flight by the butler and met on the other end by one of my Aunt Mary's people. But when they were gone, I loaded my car. Or rather the butler did. Poor man. I hope he still has a job. He thought I'd just decided to take a nice drive instead of flying. I doubt he knew much about what was really going on."

"You might be surprised. Maybe he was rooting for you."

Amazingly, Hope smiled. She rather liked the idea that the butler might have been her ally. He'd always been good to her.

Cash scrambled some eggs, and the next thing she knew she was facing a plate with a generous portion of eggs and bacon. A tall stack of buttered toast stood between them.

She sampled everything before talking again. "This is great. I need to learn how to cook."

That brought his head up.

"I know," she said, catching his surprise. "I don't know how to do some of the most important things in life. I'm a babe in the woods and I need a teacher."

"Hattie, my housekeeper, might be willing to help you out. I've found that people generally love to talk about what they do."

"If it wouldn't add to her burden. Maybe Angie and I could learn together."

"Angie may already know something about it."

Hope nodded. "I hadn't thought of that, but you're probably right. I'll ask her first."

Angie might like being a teacher to her, Hope thought. It might be one of the first steps in the right direction. "There's a lot Angie could probably teach me."

"And maybe some she shouldn't," he said humorously.

"You could say the same about me," she replied, without any humor at all. Unwed and pregnant. If she was here very long that would have to be explained to Angie. Given the dimensions of what had happened, she quailed at the very idea. It had been hard enough telling Cash, and he still couldn't grasp it.

Come to that, neither could she. From time to time, in her battered heart and brain, a thought would rise up: something else was involved, something she didn't know about. Something more than social standing, scandal and Scott's bright future.

Because it was still very hard for her to believe that her parents thought more of Scott than of her. That they refused to accept that he could have raped her. That it was more important to bury something like that than to protect her. She hadn't even asked to file charges against him. All she wanted was to end the engagement and keep her baby.

She almost put her head in her hands, but she had been doing that for too long. She had made good her escape, she was now employed, and while she still had a lot of wounds she was sure she was going to have to deal with, the important thing was to find a way to give this child a reasonably secure future. She could do that. After all, she wouldn't be the first, or last, single mother in the world.

Cash spoke. "Frankly, my first thought was that an unwed mother was exactly the wrong person to look after my daughter."

Her head snapped up. "Then I'll leave."

"Let me finish. I changed my mind. When the time is right, feel free to talk to Angie about it in whatever terms you prefer. It might be good for her to know that bad things can happen out there."

Hope felt torn. Angie had confided to her about a re-straining order, and as she heard those words it struck her that Cash hadn't heard about it. Angie knew bad things could happen out there, although maybe not the depth and degree of some of them. But the girl wasn't an innocent—certainly not the kind of innocent Hope had been at that age…or even more recently.

But she had virtually promised that she wasn't going to pass along anything Angie said—with a mental res-ervation for anything that seemed truly important for Cash to know. She had to stick to that, and a restraining order from the past against someone who had harassed the girl's mother didn't fit that bill.

"It's up to you, of course," Cash said, apparently taking her silence as reluctance. Nor could she correct that impression because it was partly true.

"Well, something's going to have to be explained to her before much longer," Hope admitted. "My jeans are getting too tight. Before long I'll be showing."

"Well, I can take care of the jeans when we go see the doc."

She shook her head. "That's not right, Cash. I have about a hundred dollars, and some things can wait until you pay me."

"Not the doc for sure." He arched his brows at her. "Some things just aren't right, Hope. Get used to it. I may not understand your family, but I know where my own values lie. Let it be, and let me do what's right."

A pretty remarkable man, she thought as she tried to help clean up after breakfast. Nearly everything was a new challenge to her, even filling a dishwasher.

That gave her some thinking to do. She had had no idea how much she had failed to learn simply by being raised in the lap of luxury. Her laundry list of ignorance was growing by leaps and bounds.

In fact, when she thought about it, she decided she had been raised worse than a prize filly and more like a hand-fed lap dog. How very humbling.

"I've got a few minutes before I have to get to work," Cash announced when they'd cleaned up. "I'll show you the barn, you can meet the horses and see where all the tack is. You *can* saddle your own horse?"

"I'm used to English saddles, but I can probably figure it out."

He surprised her with a laugh. "English, huh? None of that around here. A pommel is too useful. I'll show you. Plus, I guess I need to show you the right way to ride Western."

"What's the difference?"

"There are a couple of things. For example, we don't use the horse's mouth to guide it. No pulling on the reins."

"Then how…"

He interrupted her. "I get the idea that I'm going to need to give you a lesson first. How about we saddle one up and I'll show you? It'll be easy enough once you've tried it."

Hope grabbed her jacket and followed him to the barn. "I'm amazed. I lived in Texas but learned to ride English. I never rode Western. I never even thought about there being differences."

He flashed her that devastating smile of his. "There are. But like I said, you'll find this easy. We use neck reining instead of mouth reining, and we exert the rest of the control by shifting our weight in the saddle. In all, especially with the saddle spreading the weight out better, Western style is better for putting in a whole day. The horses don't tire as fast. You'll see."

"But don't you need to get to work?"

"This won't take long. A couple of turns around the corral and you'll have it. Angie got it pretty quickly. I just don't want her riding alone for obvious reasons. If something went wrong and we didn't know where she was, it could take a helluva long time to find her."

"And she gets home from school today around four?"

"Yeah. Kinda late to take her on much of a ride. If you can persuade her, you guys could go out for a much longer time tomorrow." He paused. "Are you sure you should be riding?"

"I had a friend who continued riding into her sixth

month. The main concern was falls. Anyway, I promised Angie. I'll be careful, just find me your laziest horse."

Hope wondered how patient Angie would be since she'd sort of promised a ride. Well, she'd find out this afternoon. In the meantime, she still needed to learn where the tack was and how to do everything, from saddling the horses to caring for them after the ride.

And if there was one thing she was determined to make clear to Angie before they even started on this venture, it was that a rider took care of her mount. Period.

Hope might not know how to cook or clean or even do laundry, but she sure as heck knew how to take care of a horse. She'd have been off the equestrian team instantly if she had refused to do it.

Besides, she enjoyed it. Caring for a horse felt rewarding in a way trips to the gym and playing tennis never would.

The Western saddle was heavier than she was used to, and Cash expressed some concern about her lifting it.

"I'm pregnant, not sick."

Another one of those smiles. Dang, the last thing she needed was for her heart to beat faster because a man smiled at her.

"I know," he said. "But lifting… We'll ask the doc. And about riding, too. In the meantime, just take it easy, okay? And do me a favor, don't fall off. This mare is as gentle as they come, but…"

"Hey, don't you want to thrill my family?" It was a poor joke, and she knew it instantly by the way his face darkened.

"No," he said shortly, and became all business from

that point. She guessed he'd become angry. She shrugged mentally. If *she* thought about it too much, she became furious. It was kind of touching that this man who had barely met her could already grow angry on her behalf.

Between her father and Scott, she had just about decided that all men were monsters. She might need to revise that a bit.

The differences in riding style were easy, as he had promised. She supposed sitting in the Western saddle acted as a reminder that she needed to change her habits. He was right, a few turns around the corral and she had mastered neck reining and shifting her weight in the saddle. Of course, he had selected a horse for her that probably was utterly patient and far smarter than any rider. That was okay, because she was pregnant and didn't need a spirited mount that might get an urge to toss her.

A half hour later he left to take care of whatever his business was, and she walked back to the house looking ahead to a pretty empty day. Hours to fill before Angie came home, and unfortunately in her rush to escape, she hadn't packed a lot of reading material. She had her ebook with her, but since her credit had been closed, she doubted she could buy anything else.

Simmering anger at her family made her stomach burn, but she was getting used to that. Shock had given way to acceptance, whether she liked it or not, but acceptance didn't ease her anger. She felt like a soiled rag that had been tossed in a trash bin by the very people who should have stood beside her. It was not an easy thing to live with.

Then there was her reaction to Cash. She barely knew the guy, but she'd already raised him in her estimation to heights once reserved for Scott. That ought to be a warning to her. Even knowing someone for years didn't mean you knew everything about them. Trust needed to be offered with great care.

Inside she found the housekeeper, Hattie, in the kitchen and introduced herself. "I'm Angie's new companion, Hope."

"Companion?" Hattie, who appeared to be in her early fifties, with graying hair and a motherly figure, scanned her from head to toe. "Good luck with that one."

Hope hesitated. "Should I get out of your way?"

Hattie shook her head and returned to pulling items out of the cupboards and fridge. "I don't mind company while I cook. Since you're living here, got anything special you want for dinner?"

"I'm fine with anything." Her mother had always made up the menus for the week with the cook, and while she was at college, she ate whatever was available in the cafeteria. The only time she had any say in her meals had been at a restaurant.

Hattie looked dubiously at her. "Even liver?"

At that, Hope's internal anger gave way to a laugh. "Not liver," she admitted.

"Knew there had to be something. There always is, if folks are honest. Cash don't much like it, neither. Now my Don could eat it every night. Lucky for me he doesn't insist on it. Pull up a chair. You look cold. Want some coffee or tea?"

A half hour later, she'd learned a lot about Hattie's life, her grown daughter and son, and the grandchild that was on the way. She couldn't help feeling envious about a life that hadn't been easy but had brought so much warmth and closeness to a family.

All the while, Hattie's hands were flying as she made

casseroles for easy heating. Hope could barely keep up with what she was doing and finally asked, "Would you teach me how to cook?"

That brought Hattie to a standstill. "You don't know how?"

"Not much. I'm okay with a microwave."

Hattie tsk-tsked and went back to stirring the contents of a bowl. "Something everyone needs to know, man and woman alike. Sure I'll teach you. Plain cooking, but good. We'll start Monday."

"Thank you."

"Ain't much to it, gal. Once you get the basics, you can do most anything you want."

"Sounds like I'll manage, then."

"Don't doubt it. Only met one woman in my life who couldn't. I swear she could burn water when she boiled it."

Hope giggled. "I probably could, too, right now."

"You look smarter than that to me."

"Then call me inexperienced. There's a lot I don't know. Like doing laundry and cleaning."

Hattie put her hands on her hips. "My. All right. As much as you want, I'll teach. Gotta be able to take care of yourself."

"Absolutely."

Hattie shook her head. "Nobody ever taught you?" Then she stopped as if she understood and muttered, "Sorry way to bring up a child, others doing everything."

"I agree. And now things have changed and I have to change, too."

Hattie seemed to accept that without question. "Monday," she said again. "I need to hurry today cuz my William and his wife will be here early, but Monday, we'll have plenty of time to turn a hand at anything you want."

"Thank you."

"Don't be thanking me. Tain't no trouble, really. I taught my own and I'll teach you. That Angie could use some teaching, too. Not my place."

"Maybe I can persuade her to join us."

Hattie snorted. "Not unless you got a magic wand."

Hope refused to let that comment cast her down. Hattie might be right, but she wasn't going to start with that assumption. She'd glimpsed something in Angie that suggested that the two of them were more alike than they'd appear on the surface. Emotions might be a greater uniter than lifestyle.

Hattie cleared out around noon, leaving enough ready-to-cook meals to carry them through the weekend. As she pulled on her jacket, she said, "Monday's laundry day. We'll cook and wash and get some floors done. Hope you're ready to work hard."

"I am."

Hattie gave her the first smile. "I like you, girl. Just having you around will be a good example."

Hope certainly hoped she was right. At the moment she had little else to go on.

Cash finished bringing the cattle in closer, most of them pregnant cows and heifers. Winter would come soon, and he needed to check them all out, make sure they looked healthy enough to get through the cold to come. Those that didn't he'd sell off. No point in feeding an animal that didn't have the stamina to make it. If any were diseased, he'd need to put them down.

Most of his newborn bulls had been sold off in the spring, but he retained a few of the youngsters as a hedge. You couldn't breed hundreds of cows without enough bulls. Come spring, he'd cull the bulls.

In the meantime, his attention was on preparing for the long winter to come. Extra nutrition, supplements and plenty of hay close by for use when ground grazing was no longer possible. His more-distant pastures were beginning to show signs of overgrazing, so the move couldn't wait. He, his three hands and his dogs, all worked a practiced dance to bring the herds home.

Overall, he was pretty pleased. It was starting to look as if this might be a very good year. His calves had brought a good price, leaving him well in the black for a change. As long as the winter didn't turn too harsh, he figured he'd have another good spring.

He finished early, and after they took care of the horses, he sent his hired hands home. Tomorrow or Monday would be soon enough to start running the cattle through the chutes to check them out. When the pace slowed a little around this place, he liked to give his men some extra time off. Lord knew, they worked hard enough when the tempo increased.

As he approached the house, however, dogs racing around him in circles excited about the coming feeding, he realized his good mood was beginning to evaporate. Angie would be home now, he reckoned, and before long there'd be some kind of trouble. The growing gray of the sky overhead seemed like an omen.

Damn, he had to stop thinking this way, feeling these things. Angie was his daughter. What's more, irritating as she could be, to allow her to turn him into the kind of man she wanted to believe he was would be a loss for both of them.

He had to remember her age, the troubles she was still trying to get past, how difficult this all was for her, and be the adult. Easier said than done, of course, when his stomach had a tendency to start knotting in anticipation.

So he turned his thoughts to Hope. At least she didn't give him heartburn. Yet. She was really nice to look at; he liked the way she reminded him that he was a man, not just a rancher, that he had ordinary needs…even if he couldn't act on them. All those gentle curves, probably augmented by her pregnancy, made his palms itch to touch her. And without makeup and that fancy hairdo, a guy could almost imagine that she was approachable.

"Hell," he muttered. Maybe she *would* give him heartburn. Under his roof, he now had a woman who was both pregnant and a rape victim. Not to mention the treatment her family had showed her. He reckoned she probably needed some professional help with all that. Who wouldn't?

Crap.

Well, it was a good reminder for him. The way Hope had been treated by her family stood like a warning flag about his relationship with Angie. He owed his daughter more than a roof, food and clothes. He just had to find a way to provide it that she wouldn't reject out of hand.

Maybe, just maybe, Hope could bridge the gap somehow. Even if she only eased Angie's isolation and anger, it would be a help.

When he got inside, he found a note from Hattie telling him what was in the freezer and fridge and a reminder that Monday was laundry day. She also told him that with an extra person, she needed to do some grocery shopping and would bring him the bill on Monday, as well.

Bless Hattie. She was a lifesaver. Once he'd started to grow his herd, taking care of the cooking and cleaning as well had become difficult. Things had started to become unmanageable, and Hattie had stepped in. She made it possible for him to occasionally take breathers in the evening. He even had a dream of someday being able to hire a foreman he could trust so he could handle more of the business end. Not that he really wanted to give up his time outside looking after things, but as his operation grew, he had to stay on top of a whole lot of clerical stuff, too. Every freaking bale of hay, every repair, every single cow had to be accounted for. It sometimes seemed as if he was being slowly turned into a bean counter.

He knew cattle, always had, but the rest of it…well, he still found himself on a steep learning curve, usually enhanced by a quarterly visit from his accountant.

He hung his hat on a peg by the back door, jacked his boots off and padded in his socks to find out what was going on in his house. It was certainly quiet.

He grabbed a cup of coffee from what appeared to be a fresh pot and went on the hunt to discover the day's disaster.

He found Hope all by herself in the living room. She held a book he recognized, one of the novels from his bookshelf. She looked up and smiled. Boy, that smile. It was nice to see on her face and made her even prettier. Her moss-green eyes were warm.

"Hi," she said. "Good day?"

"Got everything done I needed to." Which was pretty much his measure of any day. "Angie get home?"

"Shortly after four. She's upstairs."

He looked up, amazed at the quiet. "Anything happen?"

"I think she was disappointed that I suggested we

wait until morning to go riding, but it's clouding over and I didn't know how much light we'd have."

"Good decision. How'd she react?"

"About how anyone her age would." Hope bit her lower lip and closed the book she held. "Cash, I promised her that I wasn't going to spy on her. I also told her that I wasn't going to repeat my conversations with you. I'll tell you anything I think you need to be concerned about, but really, I'll never gain her trust if she feels I'm reporting every little thing to you."

"You're right." He hadn't thought about that. As he settled on his armchair, he remarked, "I was just trying to take the emotional temperature around here."

At that Hope's lovely lips pursed a bit and her eyes almost danced. "I'm sure you'll find out eventually."

"No doubt. How are *you* doing?"

"I'm fine. I hope you don't mind me borrowing a book."

"Absolutely not. Otherwise?"

She leaned forward a bit and appeared a little excited. "Hattie's going to teach me how to cook and clean."

He was startled. "And that makes you happy?"

"You bet. You have some idea how I was raised. Things have changed and it's time for me to learn how to take care of myself and my baby. It's not enough to be a pretty bauble who engages in acceptable amusements."

He turned that around in his head. "Can you tell me something?"

"If I know."

"Would you have been happy continuing that kind of life, assuming everything hadn't gone to hell with Scott?"

"Truthfully, I never really thought about it." She

shook her head a little. "I was raised to a certain life, Cash. I didn't question it. My future role was to be a wife, a mother, an adjunct to some man's career. The role grew a little when I became engaged to Scott, but it seemed important and sufficient. So I never really thought about it."

"And now? Would you go back if you could get this sorted out?"

"No."

The vehemence of her tone surprised him. "That angry?"

"Partly. But I finally realized something that probably sounds pretty stupid. Money isn't everything, and it can go away fast. The only thing you can really rely on is yourself. I have to be able to care for myself and my baby. I owe it to my child."

He nodded slowly. "But there are other things you can rely on. Like friends. Maybe not your old ones, but you might make some good new ones who will be there for you. Take me. I look pretty self-sufficient out here running a cattle ranch on my own, but I guarantee you I couldn't make it without good neighbors. They help me out a whole lot and I try to return the favor. Nobody really makes it solo. We all need community."

"I left mine behind, I guess."

"Apparently for good reason. Why couldn't you even tell your friends what was going on?"

"I didn't have any unsupervised contact with them. Because the scandal would have gotten out. I told you I was pretty much under house arrest, and it was made clear to me that I couldn't tell anyone what had happened. Spreading lies, they called it. Regardless, while it might have made me feel better to be able to talk to one of my girlfriends, I doubt I would have been believed, anyway. Scott a rapist? I can just hear the reactions."

He could well imagine them. The pair were engaged, maybe she'd misunderstood or overreacted, and yeah, that guy meant to be senator couldn't possibly have done such a thing. With everyone knowing everyone else, it would have been hard to accept. Rapists weren't people you knew and respected. They were nameless, faceless threats that emerged from the darkness.

He suspected that Hope would have been the one facing the chorus of disapproval and criticism from every direction. From what little he knew of the subject, date rape was pretty hard to prove, anyway.

So, if she'd spoken up, she still would have been the outcast, victimized all over again.

"I'm sorry," he said at last. "The dynamics were horrible, weren't they?"

She nodded. Her smile was long gone, and he had himself to blame for that. He'd brought up the ugliness, but he didn't regret it. This woman needed someone on her side, someone who would listen to her and believe her.

He had surprisingly little trouble believing her. Maybe because he didn't know Scott. Her family's actions bothered him most of all, though. Not that he had any right to judge. For screwed-up parent of the year, he probably deserved high honors, to judge by Angie. He didn't know a lot of the reasons they'd never connected when she was younger, but clearly he had failed way back and was now facing a mountain at least partly of his own making.

"You look annoyed," Hope said.

He glanced at her again and realized that given what

they had been talking about, she had no idea the direction his thoughts had taken.

"I am annoyed," he admitted. "Thinking about the way your family treated you got me thinking about Angie and our relationship. I sure screwed up something, and it started way back. It was like she didn't want to see me or spend time with me. I'd go down to Arizona for a few days to spend time with her, and it was like trying to hug an icicle. I sometimes wondered what her mother said about me."

"Was your ex angry with you?"

"Isn't that what most divorce is about? And it was my fault, I guess. My dad had died, I was trying to build up this place and pay off a load of debt and I doubt I was a very good husband. Too busy, too preoccupied, no time for fun or going places. Sandy knew ranch life, but she'd also had a life of her own before we married. Time to spend with friends and so on. That kind of blew away."

"All work and no play?"

"That's pretty much it. In all fairness, I don't think she was being too demanding, but she needed more than an absent husband, which I guess I was emotionally and mentally. After the first rush wore off, anyway. She got the bad end of the deal, left to her own resources too much. When I look back at it, it's like we were leading separate lives even before Angie was born."

"Are you always so ready to accept the blame for everything?"

He looked at her, then laughed. "Just trying to be fair."

Footsteps sounded on the stairs and their conversation froze. Moments later Angie appeared.

"Conspiring?" she asked. The question didn't sound either friendly, or like a joke.

Hope spoke first, saving Cash from having to admit he'd been talking about the girl's mother. "I was telling your dad about all the things I'm going to be learning. For one, Hattie is going to teach me to cook."

Angie remained as she was for what felt like forever, then she edged a few steps into the room. "You don't know how to cook? At all?"

"Well, I can microwave. I make mean microwave popcorn."

"That's really bad," Angie said bluntly. "Everybody knows how to cook at least some."

"Well, I'd be happy to take you as a teacher if you're willing," Hope said warmly.

"I'll think about it. When's dinner?"

"Hungry?" Cash asked. "Hattie left a meal in the fridge. Want me to heat it now?"

"I can do that."

Cash hoped astonishment didn't show on his face. Angie had never before offered to help with anything. Then the girl looked at Hope. "Come on, I'll show you how."

Cash was on the outs again, but he didn't mind. He chose to see this as a good sign. Maybe Hope would be able to go places that he couldn't, at least not yet.

Chapter Four

Dinner the night before hadn't been too bad, Hope thought as she dressed for riding the following morning. Angie had been abrupt and a bit distant as she showed Hope how to heat the casseroles, and added a bag of premixed salad fixings to a bowl with bottled dressing on the side.

During dinner, however, her iciness toward her father had been evidenced by her utter silence and her quick escape afterward, leaving Hope with an opportunity to learn how to use the dishwasher.

"I think you're having an inhibiting effect on her behavior," Cash remarked as he introduced her to the fine art of cleaning up after a meal and putting away leftovers.

"That probably won't last," Hope had responded. She wondered how long her grace period would endure.

Now they were to meet for a ride. If Angie had eaten breakfast, Hope had no idea. Cash was already gone when she got up, leaving a note that he'd left to help out a neighbor and wasn't sure when he'd be back.

The girl was waiting for her in the kitchen, dressed in jeans, cowboy boots and a jacket.

"Would you mind if I ate something first?" Hope asked.

Angie waved a hand. "Help yourself. Cereal in the cupboard beside the refrigerator, or you can make toast." Then Angie paused and an almost impish expression appeared on her face. "*Can* you make toast?" she asked.

Hope had to smile. "I may have been very privileged once, but I *did* make my own toast. I think I can handle it."

"Amazing," Angie said, then resumed her silent brooding.

Hope made her toast without a problem, and spread it with peanut butter. With a cup of tea, she joined Angie at the table.

"Is it hard getting used to a new school?" she asked, hoping she wouldn't get her head bitten off. "I never had to do it."

"It seems like there were a lot of things you never had to do before," Angie retorted.

"True," Hope agreed. "I'm not proud of it."

"No? I bet you had everything you wanted."

Hope hesitated, her heart accelerating a bit. Painful memories wanted to return, reminding her that she still had a lot to deal with. She'd been so frantic, angry and depressed since this all blew up, that she'd wound up being almost obsessive about getting away. Funny thing was, while she'd fled, she'd taken most of her troubles along with her and added a few more. But staying had been out of the question.

"Well?" Angie demanded.

"For a long time I thought I did," Hope said carefully.

"What changed?"

"I grew up. The hard way." God, she didn't like to talk about this, and talking about it with a thirteen-year-old seemed cruel. She didn't want to destroy Angie's illusions unnecessarily, but on the other hand, maybe Angie had already had enough of them dashed. She'd mentioned a restraining order, and then there was her mother's unexpected death. She wondered if Cash even knew about the order, or that Angie had been afraid because of it.

"Well?" Angie prodded.

"Short story," Hope finally said. "I discovered the man I was engaged to was a monster, and I discovered my family cared more about him than me."

Angie didn't speak for a long time while Hope nibbled at her toast.

"I get it," she said finally. "Except my mother loved me."

"I'm sure she did."

"My dad doesn't."

"You may change your mind about that. He's certainly worried about you."

"Yeah, enough to get someone else to keep an eye on me."

Hope didn't know how to answer that. Just as she took another bite of her toast, Angie spoke again.

"That restraining order I told you about?"

"Yes?"

"It was because I told my mom that her boyfriend was trying to do dirty things with me."

The toast in Hope's mouth turned to sawdust. She couldn't even speak as an Arctic wind seemed to blow through her. At last she grabbed a paper napkin and spit out the toast as best she could. "Did he…?"

"I guess not. But he was sure on his way."

"I am so sorry." Words were useless. Hope's heart cramped so painfully that it was hard to draw breath. "So sorry," she said again, pushing her plate away. "And so glad your mother believed you. Sometimes mothers don't."

Angie lifted her head, and her dark eyes bored into Hope. "Is that what happened to you? Your mother didn't believe you?"

"Nobody believed me." Hope squeezed her eyes shut, battling down the rising agony for Angie and herself.

"Stupid people," Angie said. "Stupid, stupid." Then she jumped up from the table and dashed out the back door as if trying to escape what she had just said.

Hope struggled against her own pain. Grabbing her jacket, she hurried after Angie, trusting that a little jogging wouldn't hurt the baby. How would she know? She hadn't even talked to a doctor yet. Cash was right—she needed to see one soon.

But worry about her child took a backseat to her concern about Angie for the moment. She hoped the girl didn't try to run off because she had no idea how far she could follow, or if she could even keep up. If Angie turned up missing…

But Angie was waiting outside the barn, her icy mask again firmly in place. When Hope thought about all the pain that mask was hiding, she figured her own story hardly compared. Yes, she'd been raped. Yes, nobody believed her. Yes, they wanted her to get rid of her child or marry her rapist, but she was an adult. Angie was not. She seemed like such a young, small package to be holding so much inside her.

"You *can* ride?" Angie asked acidly.

"I thought I told you I could. I used to be on a team and compete, actually." The words came out of her breathlessly after her trot. "But you're still going to have to help me. Riding Western style is new to me."

"It's easy, especially on the horses Dad lets me ride."

"That's good to know."

Angie looked her over. "You're out of shape. That wasn't a very long run."

A little bubble of nearly hysterical laughter rose in Hope. Yes, she was probably out of shape, but mostly because of a baby and too much confinement. "I'll work on it."

Inside the barn they were greeted by one of the hired hands, a man called Ed. He was busy forking fresh hay into the stalls.

"A visit from two lovely ladies," he said with a smile.

"We're going riding," Angie said.

"Glad to help."

Angie looked about to rebel, and Hope stepped in quickly. "Can we try, Ed? You can watch to make sure we do everything right, especially since I'm not used to Western tack, but I was taught every horsewoman takes care of her own mount and tack."

Ed nodded approvingly. "It's true. Horses before self," he opined. Then he said quietly, "Not Brutus, Angie. No one rides him but your dad. Okay?"

"I need something gentle," Hope said swiftly. "It's been a while."

Angie didn't look too happy at being nudged toward the horses that Cash had suggested yesterday. Hope was sure the girl wanted to gallop with the wind, but she gathered Angie wasn't all that experienced yet, and besides, she didn't know if it would be safe for herself.

"We'll graduate upward," Hope remarked to Angie as they began to saddle their mounts. "I need baby steps right now."

"You need baby steps for a lot of things," Angie groused, but at least going for a ride seemed more important than riding the most spirited mount in the stalls.

Hope didn't disagree with her. "I love horses. I've always loved horses. Don't you?"

Angie's response was a grunt, but once they began to ride away from the barn her mood seemed to settle and improve.

It was, Hope thought, hard to remain upset about much while swaying on the back of a good-tempered horse under a cobalt sky on a brisk day.

But she had a lot to think about now, and she wondered how much she should share with Cash. She also felt closer to Angie than she would have believed possible just a day ago. They had a lot in common, and she chewed that over as she enjoyed the wonderful feeling of riding again.

The girl needed a confidante, a friend. Someone to whom she could open up that pain so tightly locked in her, pain that right now emerged only as anger.

But who was she to talk? She was harboring a tight knot of anger, pain and fear herself, and she hadn't dared share it even with a friend. Sometimes it was easier to talk to a stranger. Cash had been right about that.

But apart from talking, she wasn't even thinking. Not really. She'd been reacting for months now, but never dealing with the reality of all that had happened to her. It was as if she remained in a state of shock, hardly absorbing the events of her own life, just putting one foot in front of the other as each new wrinkle arose.

She was living in a self-protective crouch. That had to change.

Angie withdrew after their ride. She did stay to help with currying and cleaning the horses' hooves, which would surely please her father. It probably helped that Ed showed up to compliment her on the job she was doing, and it might have helped some that Hope took it as a given that they would care for their own mounts.

But then Angie vanished into her room, appearing only once to grab a sandwich and some chips before quickly disappearing without a word. Hope could only imagine what she was doing. From time to time she thought she heard the sounds of a TV, possibly a movie. The girl needed more in her life, but Hope couldn't imagine how to add it.

Of course, she needed more herself. Being under house arrest at home, there had still been things to occupy her. Here there was nothing familiar to her, no way to amuse herself other than reading or TV. She was used to a busier life, and had assumed Angie would keep her running except for when she was in school.

Now time hung heavy on Hope's hands, a new experience for her. She'd left behind her art projects, the hours she had once liked to spend designing clothes or painting landscapes. She had no friends to call and chat with, no golf outings, none of the multitude of ways she had filled her days.

Which left her plenty of time to think about what had happened to her, and to begin to suspect that a busy life wasn't necessarily a full life.

Yes, she'd volunteered with charities, but her role had

always been above it all in a sense. She organized food for the poor and homeless; she didn't actually cook it or dole it out. She sat on boards, never getting into the nitty-gritty. Most of the time she'd mainly been a recognizable name on the letterhead and a donor.

In short, she was used to being busy, but unfamiliar with herself. The thought jolted her. How little time she'd had to really discover who she was. From earliest childhood, she'd been entertained and occupied. She'd learned a whole lot about some things and nothing about herself, really.

Would the real Hope Conroy please stand up? The bitter question floated into her awareness. She was, as the saying went, a person doing, not a person being. There had always been a goal, a task, an appearance to make. Take riding, for example. Never before today had she just meandered on horseback. No, she had always been involved in training of herself and her mount.

So today had been a first for her, riding with no goal, no destination, no purpose other than to enjoy herself.

On impulse, she went upstairs and knocked on Angie's door. She heard the TV volume go down and Angie say querulously, "Yeah?"

Hope opened the door and peered in. Angie sat against a big pile of pillows on her bed, surrounded by what looked like schoolbooks. "Do you know yourself?"

Angie nearly gaped. "What do you mean?"

"I was just wondering. Because among the many things I don't know, I just realized I don't know myself."

Angie half shrugged. "What's to know? I'm just me."

"I'm not even sure who me is, if you get my meaning. I think I'm a mess."

"Who isn't," Angie said glumly. "You need a shrink."

"Maybe so. Sorry I bothered you." Hope closed the door quietly and started back downstairs. What had possessed her to go up there and ask such a stupid question? She was sure most people would have gaped at her.

But then, before she reached the top of the steps, she heard a door open behind her.

"Hope?" Angie's voice reached her and she turned. "You need someone to talk to?"

"A shrink, probably." But the offer touched her. "Thanks, Angie. It's kind of disturbing to realize I've never had the time to figure myself out."

Angie hesitated. "Do any of us?" Then she disappeared back into her room.

Good question, Hope thought as she continued her way downstairs. A very good question.

By the end of the week, the days had settled into a rhythm for Hope. Hattie came on Monday and Wednesday and gave her lessons in cooking and a good directed workout with cleaning. There was an interesting moment with Hattie, though.

"Hope?" she said as they made their way to the first bathroom. "You're pregnant."

It wasn't a question. Startled, Hope froze. "Does it show?"

"Only to eyes that can see. I don't want you handling these bathroom chemicals. I use the strong stuff and I'm not sure it's safe. You check with the doctor and see, okay?"

So Hope gave up on cleaning the bathrooms and settled for vacuuming, which soon started to feel like an almost Zen escape. It was certainly something she could do adequately.

Angie didn't create any more scenes, although she

remained cocooned in frost. Cash seemed to be working most of his waking hours, although he kept saying things would lighten up soon, once he had everything ready for winter.

When she remarked that she needed more to do while Angie was at school, he guided her into his office. "Can you do data entry? I take a lot of notes. If you can read my handwriting, I'd sure like to not have to type it in. I'm ham-fingered when it comes to typing."

Inevitably, she looked at his hands and noticed with a twinge of longing how strong they looked. Her reaction startled her and was utterly unwelcome. First of all, this man was her boss. But more importantly, she knew full well that she hadn't dealt with her rape. Even if she was still capable of feeling desire, she suspected that at the first touch she'd fly into a panic.

She dragged her gaze back to the computer as he explained the first of the things he needed her to do in the morning, but she couldn't drag her awareness back. She'd noticed before that he was an attractive man, but having him lean over her as she sat at his desk made her acutely aware of her own longings. One of his hands rested on the back of her chair as he leaned toward the keyboard to punch keys, showing her how to do things.

She felt surrounded by him, and two competing tensions rose in her. His masculine scent filled her nostrils; her insides ached to know the pleasure he might give her. At the same time fear caused her heart to hammer. Her mouth turned dry as sand, and her palms grew damp. She froze.

All of a sudden, he straightened. "I'm sorry," he said, and walked out.

She remained frozen for what felt like an endless time, but was probably less than a minute. Caught in a web of conflicting needs and fears, her brain reacted like a startled deer. Then his words penetrated.

Her limbs moved again and she jumped up. She found him in the living room, sitting in his easy chair, staring off into space. He barely glanced her way when she entered the room.

She licked her lips and managed to speak a few words over the hammering of her heart. Everything warned her not to pursue this, but she couldn't ignore it, either. "Sorry for what?"

"You were getting tense. I could feel it. Then it suddenly struck me that a woman who was raped only a few months ago probably didn't want any man within arm's distance. So I apologized."

He still wasn't looking at her. She edged into the room, wondering just how honest she dared to be. But this man had been kind to her, giving her a job and a place to live, and tomorrow morning he was even taking her to a doctor…at his own expense. She owed him something more than evasions, and certainly she hadn't yet broken the wall of ice his daughter had erected, a wall that had troubled him enough to reach out for help. He could, after all, have just shrugged it away, an act far less cruel that what her parents had done to her.

She edged in closer and perched on the edge of the sofa. It was a serviceable piece of furniture, like most of the furnishings around here, showing some wear but still functional. She ran her hand over the arm, thinking of the differences between her past and this man's. He'd worked for everything he had, and it wasn't a whole lot. In one week, she'd come to know just how hard and time-consuming that work was. To keep things going, he had three hired hands and a part-time cook and housekeeper. All four must stretch his budget, but for the sake of his daughter he'd taken on yet another employee, someone he hoped might at least give his daughter a friend.

"Did you pay child support?" she asked. The question popped out of her, and startled her as much as him. Finally he looked at her.

"Of course," he said.

"It wasn't always easy, was it?"

"Important stuff is rarely easy. Some years it was easier than others. What does it matter? Angie needed it."

"Did they live better in Arizona than they did here?"

"From what I saw, but that depends on what you consider better. It was important to Sandy to be close to other people. She was ranch raised, so I didn't expect it to become a problem, but after Angie was born, her mobility was reduced. She couldn't get to town as easily, couldn't see as much of her friends. I think she started to suffer from loneliness. And maybe I was a fool. I was working all the time, just like now. I assumed too much, I guess."

"But you don't have a choice about how much you work."

"Not really. Not if I want to keep this place and pay the bills."

She turned that around in her mind, realizing that in a way he'd just warned her. Why he should find that necessary she didn't know. After all, she was just here to look after his daughter. She didn't even know how long he'd want to keep her around.

"What about you?" he asked abruptly. "Always looking for something else to work on... You about done with the isolation?"

"Are you asking if I want to leave?"

"Well, you've had a week of it and don't seem happy just hanging around."

"Funny you should put it that way." She sighed. "It's true I'm used to being busy. But there's all kinds of busy, and I can see a whole lot of things around here that I'd do if I knew how. I don't have to sit around staring out the windows. I don't want to. But I'm happy working with Hattie and spending time with Angie, and I'm sorry if I overstepped by asking if there was something more I could do."

"You didn't overstep."

Silence fell again. She nearly sighed, realizing for the first time that this kind and generous man had nearly as many walls as his daughter. Sandy's desertion must have hit him deeply. He was already looking for reasons for her to want to leave.

"Well, I don't want to leave," she announced. "I'm enjoying learning new things, but most of all I enjoy feeling useful."

His brow arched. "You didn't feel useful before?"

"Not very often. I was a decoration, a name to be used, a social butterfly who was supposed to make the right connections with the right people. For a politician's wife, that would all be useful, but that's not going to happen now, and I'm kind of surprised how little I miss it. There was a pointlessness to it that I didn't even realize. At least not until I started thinking about this baby's future. I wonder if I would have remained stupidly oblivious if matters hadn't blown up."

He didn't answer for a while. She couldn't tell if he was thinking about what she had said, or about something else, like Angie. Or his ex. Sandy had probably left him with a lot of unanswered questions about the kind of man he was.

She sure had a lot of questions about what kind of woman she was. Had been, would become. Reflecting on her past didn't make her very proud, though. Some part of herself had begun to feel she hadn't been put in this world with no purpose other than to fulfill the expectations of others.

But maybe that was depressed thinking. She supposed Cash could be sitting over there contemplating the same questions, like sacrificing everything to this ranch. What was the point?

Maybe that was the wrong question to ask.

When he didn't speak again, she gathered her courage and addressed the issue that had caused her to come in here. "I'm sorry I was getting tense," she said. "I wasn't afraid of you. You don't need to worry about that."

"Maybe *you* should," he said, his mouth twisting.

Her heart climbed right into her throat and began pounding, almost choking her.

"You see," he said, "while I know I have more self-control than your Scott did, and I'd never touch you without permission, I still find myself wanting you."

The bald admission stole the rest of her breath. All she could do was stare at him blankly, unable to even react.

"So, that's part of what I was apologizing for. I'll keep my distance, but you might as well know. Now that you do, if you get uneasy about staying here, just tell me. I'll see that you leave here with enough in your pocket to go somewhere else you can feel safer."

With that he rose, bade her good-night and climbed the stairs.

Stunned, Hope sat on in solitude, her mind spinning,

her heart filled with his blunt admission. Astonishingly, she didn't at all feel like running.

Well, that had sure torn it, Cash thought as he stood in the dark in his bedroom staring out over a peaceful night. He could see the shadows of his herd, clustered for the night, the more swiftly moving shadows of the dogs as they patrolled. Above all, a diamond-studded moonless sky seemed to shower grace.

Inside, he felt anything but peaceful or grace-filled. For the past week he'd been struggling with his desire for Hope, but that didn't mean he needed to tell her. Warn her. He knew the limits of his self-control, and they were far beyond any threat Hope posed to them. He'd never touch her unless she wanted it.

But having her around was kind of like having a burr under his saddle, and she might as well know it. She might better understand if he got irritable or if he withdrew inexplicably, the way he had tried to do tonight. Or she might move on. He'd be sorry if she did, because if nothing else she seemed to be pouring some oil on the troubled waters of his relationship with Angie. Yeah, the deep freeze was still turned up high, but the fights had disappeared. He wondered how long that would last. Icy civility was easier to deal with than the rages and rants.

None of which indicated that Angie was getting any better, and that was another thing that gnawed at him ceaselessly. Damn, he was surrounded by women who were apt to drive him to the edge of madness.

He should have been laughing at himself, but tonight that didn't seem easy. He'd thought he was hiring Hope because he felt sorry for her, and because he wanted a woman closer to Angie's age. Hattie sure hadn't made any breakthroughs with the girl. There might even be too many years between Angie and Hope to be real buddies, but maybe there weren't so many that they couldn't get closer. Like sisters, maybe.

At least that's what he had told himself. Now he wondered if his libido had played a major part in his decision. He hoped not. The woman had been raped and impregnated. She'd been through hell with her fiancé and her family. He hoped he was a better man than to hire her just because she turned him on.

Didn't matter, anyway, he told himself brutally. Even if she felt an attraction to him, even if she could overcome her experience with Scott, where would that get them? He'd still be the same work-all-the-time rancher and she'd probably get really tired of this place, especially come winter. Right now it was all new and fresh. Give it time and she'd probably become as discontented as Sandy had.

If a ranch-bred wife couldn't handle this life, how could someone who'd once apparently had everything in the world at her fingertips?

And this was a truly stupid line of thought. The woman had been here a week. What was he thinking, imagining catastrophes in a future that would probably never happen?

Shaking his head, he finally turned from the window and stripped. Until Angie's arrival, he'd always slept naked, but these days he invariably pulled on a pair of sweatpants in case something happened in the night.

The time might come when she might need him. Anything was possible, and when it came, if it came, he hoped he was ready. That he did and said all the right things.

All these years he'd wondered why she hadn't let him

close, even when she was tiny. He'd blamed it on his every visit being a visit with a stranger. Every meeting between them meant they had to start all over again. It wasn't enough to be a dad two or three times a year.

He got that, but what he'd never wanted to admit, except in the depths of his heart, was how much that hurt. She was his *daughter*. He should have been part of her life, and she of his. He'd tried to get her to spend summers or holidays here but she had always refused.

So now she was here for good, like it or not, and apparently angry about everything. He couldn't blame her for most of it, but he sure wished he had some kind of magic wand that could at least give them a chance to make a connection.

As for Hope...well, young though she was, that was one brave woman. A lot of backbone stiffened that pretty package and he admired that.

But he was certain her life didn't lie here. Eventually she'd be ready to move on, and he'd encourage her to find her own way. He was sure she could. So this longing that kept plaguing him needed to be stamped out. Doused. Quashed.

Neither of them needed this complication, and after what he'd said tonight, he wouldn't be a bit surprised to wake in the morning and find her waiting with packed bags when he was supposed to take her to the doctor.

He rolled over, punching the pillow. He was used to being alone, so why did he suddenly feel lonely? Why the craving for things he couldn't have?

He didn't have the answers. So what was new? As far as he could tell, pushing closer to forty hadn't made him one whit wiser.

Chapter Five

In the morning, shortly after Angie had caught the school bus, Cash helped Hope into his truck and set out for town.

"Aren't you too busy to take me to the doctor?" she asked.

"I have time."

"But…" Again she hesitated. "Maybe we should have driven Angie to school?"

"I didn't want to answer questions about where I was taking you. It's up to you to decide when and how you want to tell her you're pregnant."

"I wish I didn't have to tell her at all." Her hands curled into fists as another wave of anger at Scott rolled through her, along with a contradictory excitement about having a baby. That excitement hadn't had room in her thoughts before, mainly because she'd been so overwhelmed by what had happened, by the threats that had shockingly become a daily diet, by a need to escape both marriage to her tormentor and any possibility of losing this child.

She'd been hunkered in survival mode, but even as the anger soured her mouth, she realized she was happy about her child. *Talk about a mishmash*, she thought, unable to explain it even to herself.

For the past couple of years, she'd been looking forward to getting married. The idea of children had been put on hold. Both she and Scott had agreed they should wait a year or two before starting a family. Time, he had said, for the two of them to settle in with each other and enjoy their relationship before dealing with the demands of children.

Except now she wondered about that. The demands of children? Was that his innate selfishness speaking, because she now knew just how selfish he could be. Of course, she understood that having a child would change a lot, but in their circles it didn't have to change that much. Everyone had some kind of nanny, and Scott must have expected they would have one.

She admonished herself to stop thinking about Scott. No point in it. She had thought she knew him; now it was clear she never had. Asking herself questions about him and why he had done some things would never get her any answers. Not now. Maybe if she'd still been with him, asking him would only have revealed that he didn't have any answers, anyway.

She certainly had few about herself. Trying to get out of her own head, at least temporarily, she turned her attention back to Cash. "So you think it was being confined by having a small child that made your wife leave? But she must have known all along how hard you have to work."

"What is this? Therapy?"

She might have withdrawn and apologized, except his tone had betrayed amusement.

"We dated when my dad was still alive and managing the ranch. So I had more time. Never occurred to me I might be raising false expectations. Anyway, about the time Angie was born, my dad had a serious heart attack. He became unable to do any real work, so it all fell to me. Then a few months later he died in his sleep. That left me to handle everything. So between all the work of a new baby and me being occupied pretty much every hour of the day, I'm not surprised she felt abandoned."

"You're making excuses for her."

"No, I've just had a lot of time to think about what went wrong. I take my full share of the blame."

She didn't see much blame under the circumstances. It wasn't as if he had set out to create the situation, and as he had remarked, Sandy was ranch-bred. She must have had some idea of the work involved.

Still. Hope closed her eyes and allowed memories to come. She and Scott hadn't been living in each others' pockets. Throughout their dating and engagement, their relationship had been reserved for weekends when one or both of them didn't have to be somewhere else. Her own parents had lived that way, meeting at social gatherings, or over breakfast, then going their own ways. It had seemed normal to her.

But Sandy had been in a different situation, she realized. Her own parents had always been busy with other people, whether it was her dad going to work, or her mother to committee meetings or out with friends. Sandy had had none of that.

Hope sighed quietly, the sound lost in the rattle and roar of the truck as it bounced over bad roads. The future, she reminded herself, couldn't be predicted. Cash couldn't have known that his father would die at probably the worst possible time for his marriage. Maybe it wouldn't have fallen apart if Cash had taken over once Angie was older and Sandy could get around more.

Or maybe other things had been going on, things he didn't know about. Regardless, marriage was a leap of faith no matter how you felt about your partner. She could only be glad that she had discovered Scott's ugly side before she'd taken her vows. If she thought she'd faced opposition the way things were, she could only imagine what would have happened if she'd decided she had to get away after they were married. Especially if he had been in the middle of a campaign.

Maybe it was all for the best.

As they pulled into the parking lot at the doctor's office, she became nervous. This was going to be hard. Hard to explain why she hadn't seen a doctor yet. She didn't want to go through all that again. Didn't want to have to explain the rape. She also feared that she was going to get deservedly scolded for her negligence. But mostly, she realized as her hands cramped into fists, she was worried about her baby. She'd been able to endure this long because so far she hadn't had any obvious problems. She'd shepherded a few friends through their pregancies, and had reassured herself that if anything was seriously wrong she would get some sign. Now she wasn't able to delude herself any longer.

Cash once again proved to be remarkably perceptive. "What's wrong?" He turned off the ignition and swiveled to face her.

"How did you get to be so good at reading people?"

"Am I? Maybe it comes from having to pay such close attention to the signals my animals make. I don't know. So what tightened you up?"

"I'm nervous. I'm afraid he'll find something wrong. I'm afraid of getting yelled at for not having seen a doctor sooner."

"Brad isn't like that. You'll see. His primary interest is going to be ensuring that you have a healthy pregnancy."

He climbed out and came around to help her out. "Deep breath," he said with a smile. "You'll like him, and next time you won't be worried about seeing him."

Dr. Brad, as he preferred to be called, turned out to be as nice as Cash promised. He didn't question her delay in seeing a doctor but talked to her gently, checked her out and assured her that everything seemed fine. She left his office with a bottle of prenatal vitamins, an appointment for next month and a question about whether she wanted a sonogram. She refused, explaining she couldn't afford it.

"We can do something about that," he said with a smile. "Think about it."

Cash paid the for the examination, leaving her truly embarrassed. "Take it out of my pay," she asked when they were back in his truck.

"Like hell. You need to be building a nest egg for that baby. Next stop Freitag's Mercantile. You need either some looser clothes or some maternity clothes."

"But…"

"Hush. It's the least I can do, and I'm not planning to go overboard."

Freitag's both fascinated her and surprised her. It smelled as old as it looked, with creaky wood floors from an earlier era. She wasn't swarmed by well-dressed women only too eager to find her the "perfect" outfit, but faced instead with crowded racks and stacks on long tables. One saleswoman in her fifties pointed them to the maternity clothes where the selection was adequate but hardly eye-catching. There were some business clothes, but mostly these were clothes designed for ranchers' wives. Businesslike in another way, she supposed. Plenty of jeans, heavy-duty slacks and tops that seemed not to want to get in the way with so much as a ruffle.

She kind of liked it. *Practical.* A word she had to learn all over again because now it had a new meaning in her life.

At Cash's insistence, she was able to find several pairs of jeans with stretch panels on the front that fit, and five maternity tops that she liked. They looked more like work shirts, and that appealed to her, snaps down the front, a couple in chambray and others in plaids she liked.

Cash disappeared when the kindly saleswoman started pushing undergarments on her. "Whatever she needs," he said, heading for the front of the store.

In the fitting room, as she tried on bras because her cup size was increasing, the woman said, "I didn't know Cash had a new lady friend."

At once Hope's cheeks flamed, and for the first time she wondered what kind of gossip this little trip might cause. She could easily imagine that a small town like this might have quite a gossip mill. Why not? The circles she had used to run in certainly had.

"I'm not with Cash," she said. "I just started working for him. We only met a week ago."

That brought an arched brow, but no more questions emerged from the woman. Now she guessed they'd indulge in all kinds of speculation about her, but she didn't care about that. She knew no one here, and had no idea how long she would remain. Cash could easily let her go at any time. Or she might decide she needed to move on.

Angie would be the determining factor in that, she thought as Cash paid for her purchases. If she couldn't get through to the girl in some way, Cash might decide he needed someone else. So far, though, he hadn't seemed to expect a miracle, but it had been little more than a week.

Back at the ranch, Cash grabbed a couple of peanut butter sandwiches then headed to work. Hope went upstairs to change into her new clothes, and breathed a sigh of relief that the waistband of her jeans no longer bound her tightly.

But as she was jamming her feet into her riding boots, she had a thought. If that woman at Freitag's gossiped, if anyone had seen Cash taking her into the gynecologist's office—well, Angie would probably hear about it soon. And not in a nice way.

She straightened, staring at the wall, feeling trepidation rise. She would have to tell Angie, and telling Angie was going to be hard. The girl wasn't a total naïf, but this? This might ruin the tenuous strands that were just beginning to grow. Angie could easily feel she had been lied to by Hope's concealment of the truth for the past ten days.

A few cusswords that she had never been allowed to use floated into her brain.

For a fact, her realities had been shifting so rapidly that she wondered if she was dealing at all. For so long she'd been drifting along, her biggest problem the occasional disagreement with a friend. Life had been like a lovely, warm river, just carrying her from one new vista to the next. There had been nothing important to worry about, ever. Well, except for what others thought of her. That had been drilled into her from her earliest age.

That reality had shattered after Scott's attack. Escape had led her into a whole new reality, different from anything that had come before. She needed to wrap her head around it, and start becoming proactive in her own life, at least as much as she could.

Yes, fighting with her parents to save her baby and not marry Scott had been proactive. So had running away, but since she had arrived here she seemed to be looking for a way to drift again. Looking for additional work to do around here didn't necessarily mean she was coping with anything. She had to make plans of some kind for a future.

She had to deal with Angie. Somehow. She had to deal with Cash. His admission last night that he wanted her had shaken her to her core, surprising her in part because she hadn't been horrified, afraid or anything else she would have anticipated after being raped. Astonishing her, because her own response to him had been nagging at her only to be swiftly dismissed. Now it was hard to dismiss because he reciprocated.

A small, wild urge arose in her, whispering that she should take advantage of her desire and Cash's to find out if she was still essentially okay after Scott, or if she'd run screaming at a man's touch.

Well, that wouldn't do at all. Not at all. It wouldn't be fair to Cash to use him like a crash test dummy. Plus, it would be totally stupid. She had no surety of a life here, so why wreck the goodness she'd found by taking it further? Additionally, she might risk cementing Angie's anger forever.

She was touched, though, that Cash had told her that. He must have guessed she'd suspect it sooner or later, so he'd promised she could leave at any time and he'd make sure she had the wherewithal to do so. A remarkable man in so many ways. He had given her a chance when she most needed it, and now he was caring for her like a member of his family.

The things Cash had done for her meant far more than the dozens of red roses, the fancy restaurants, the expensive plays and parties Scott had showered on her. Scott had indulged her with just about anything money could buy, but he hadn't showed her the respect she deserved. Cash had probably seriously dented his bank account with the doctor's visit and the clothes just this morning, but asked nothing in return. His gift to her was the greater by far, and the more so because he hardly knew her and expected nothing more from her than that she do the job he had hired her for.

Scott had all kinds of expectations for her. That she be available when he needed her to go to some function with him. That she find ways to make new connections for him in political circles. Once, the one time they had really fought before the rape, he'd even suggested she needed to step up her workouts at the gym because he thought she'd put on a few pounds. As it happened, she hadn't and had been infuriated.

God, he'd made her feel like a utensil, a wind-up doll to go in whatever direction he wanted.

And she'd been too stupid to realize it. Sitting on the edge of the bed, she looked back gloomily and then snorted when she realized that he'd probably have been after her to have plastic surgery by the time she was thirty to correct any signs of aging. Oh, yeah, he would have. The first question he'd always asked when they were out in daylight was, "Did you remember your sunblock?"

She got that Texas could age a woman fast if she wasn't careful. The strong sun, the heat, the wind... That had been drilled into her like everything else. But to be asked by her fiancé? At the time she had thought he was just caring for her, but now she didn't believe it.

Shaking her head, she went to her closet and pulled out her makeup kit. She was as outfitted in that department as any model, but she hadn't at all minded skipping the ritual since she got here. Yes, she still put on her sunblock, but left the rest of it in her bag.

Frankly, she thought she looked younger without all that paint, but she had an idea for it, and a girl of just the right age to love it.

Something she could try to do with Angie.

Smiling again she headed downstairs. Hattie had been bustling about when they got back and she could help with that. Then when Angie came home... Nodding to herself, her smile deepened.

Cash got back to the house just in time for dinner. Hope and Angie had heated it and set the table, and it turned into another quiet, if frigid, meal. He figured it was a good sign that Angie was helping a bit, and he wondered if Hope's restrained and polite behavior was rubbing off on the girl. She could choose a worse role model, he supposed. Angie's table manners had even improved.

"Leave the dishes," Hope said when he rose and started to clear his place. "Angie and I will take care of them."

To his amazement, Angie didn't argue. What the hell? For four months she'd refused to do a damn thing to help around here, and all she had seemed interested in was being able to ride. Now this? Improvement by osmosis?

"I know you still have work to do," Hope said. "Go on. We'll have fun."

Angie looked a little mutinous, he thought as he headed for his office. He wondered what would happen after he left the kitchen. Outright war?

But then he heard something that caused him to pause in the hallway. Hope said, "I have a surprise for you after we get the kitchen cleaned."

Surprise? He didn't know if he liked the sound of that. Maybe Hope was going to tell her about the pregnancy. If so, shouldn't he be nearby to help deal with it? Then it struck him that nothing about Hope so far indicated that she wanted to cause Angie any more problems. He might just turn into a problem if he was there. Especially since Angie was barely tolerating him, for all her open hostility had been controlled.

Sighing, he entered his office but left the door open, wanting to hear as much as he could of what was going on. Damn, he felt as if he was being cut out of his own life, not that that was fair. He'd been cut out of Angie's for quite a while.

"What's the surprise?" Angie demanded once the dishwasher was full and the casserole dishes had been washed.

Hope smiled. "You have to promise to listen to me on this. I've had bunches of experience so I won't mislead you, okay?"

Angie, still looking sour despite the spark of interest in her eyes, nodded. "Okay."

Hope ran upstairs and got her big makeup case. When

she returned to the kitchen carrying it, Angie eyed it curiously, the sourness disappearing from her face.

"You're thirteen," Hope said. "Time to learn about makeup. But you have to promise me something."

"What's that?"

"That you won't wear it to school without your dad's permission. And that you won't overdo it. The secret of makeup is for it to look so natural it doesn't stand out."

"Then why wear it?"

"Well, you don't have to. You're pretty enough as you are. But it can add a glow to your face if you do it right. You want people to wonder why you look so good without them knowing it's because you've done a few little things, okay?"

"It's like a secret?"

"Close to it. As we get older, we seem to need a little more of it, but at your age...well, you've already got all the beauty of youth. You don't need to hide it—you want to highlight it."

All resistance had vanished from Angie's face and her excitement became obvious as Hope opened the large case and displayed its contents. Expensive cosmetics, once de rigueur for Hope, became a young girl's dream.

Giggling and laughter, such an unusual sound in this house, drew Cash back down the hall, and he peered around the corner to see what was going on.

A fancy lighted mirror stood on his kitchen table, and Hope and Angie were busy with big brushes and cakes that he recognized as makeup. An instant resistance awoke in him. Angie was too young. Then he realized she wasn't too young at all, and Hope was gently encouraging her to keep it light, not to hide her natural beauty.

It also became quickly clear that they were experimenting, hence the giggles.

"Now I look like a clown," Angie tittered.

Hope passed her a pad from a jar. "Not quite, but close. See what I mean about too much?"

Angie took the pad and wiped away the stuff around her eyes. "Just this or all of it?"

Hope leaned back and looked. "All of it. I was wrong about the base color. You don't want to look like you just got jaundice."

Angie flipped a switch and the lighting on the mirror dimmed. "It doesn't look so bad in this light."

"But you're not going out at night. Let's get back to daytime. Right now that's mostly when you'd want to wear it."

Cash stepped back and returned to his office, trying not to make the floorboards creak. The laughter followed him, and he wound up smiling. Maybe that young woman could help his daughter, after all.

He resumed his seat and tried to focus on his work, but instead his thoughts drifted to Hope. His desire for her just kept erupting into his awareness like an unpredictable volcano.

Suck it up, he told himself. The woman was pregnant and recently raped. He'd almost bet that had more to do with her nervousness this morning about seeing the doctor than fear of a scolding.

But whatever she had feared this morning, tonight she was bringing Angie out of her shell. He just hoped it would last and not disappear the instant she saw him again. If it took letting his daughter wear makeup to school, then he was prepared to allow it. That girl needed something to feel good about.

"I didn't know it took so much practice," Angie said an hour or so later as they were cleaning up.

"It takes lots of practice," Hope agreed. "Finally it gets to the point where it's almost automatic, but at first it's lots of work. We can practice every night if you want, after you get your homework done."

"I need to talk Dad into getting me my own makeup."

"I have a ton of it. You're welcome to keep whatever you use after the practice is done."

"Really?" Angie's eyes lit up. "But what about you?"

"I don't think I'm ever again going to wear so much makeup. I kind of like not having it on."

"Why?"

"I don't know exactly. Maybe it's partly that now I don't have to be afraid to touch my face. Or maybe it's just the new me. Come on, let's see what your dad thinks of the new you."

Angie's face shadowed immediately. "He won't like it. He thinks I'm a kid still. I bet he says I can't wear it to school."

"Maybe so. But you keep getting older, right?"

But even Hope felt trepidation. She had done this without clearing it with Cash, and he wouldn't be the first father in the world who didn't want his young daughter wearing makeup. In fact, he might be furious. "I'll get him."

"Just don't tell him why. You said it had to be almost invisible, so let's see if it is."

Oh, great, thought Hope. There was a difference between invisible and none. To her it was obvious Angie was wearing some makeup. Not anything strong or glaring, but clearly she had done something to her face.

She headed down the hall and found Cash's door open. He was staring at a computer screen. "Got a moment, Cash?"

"Sure." He turned his chair and smiled. "It sounded like you two were having a great time."

"Girl stuff. And yes, we were."

He stood and followed her down the hall. Except for Hope's case, all sign of the makeup was gone.

Angie was leaning against the counter, her arms folded as if she expected trouble, but she lifted her face defiantly. In her eyes, Hope could see her eagerness for approval. She hoped Cash could, as well.

But somehow he handled it beautifully. "Angie! Did you change your hair or something? You look different, but I like it."

"It's makeup," she answered defiantly, but the hope blooming on her face was almost painful to behold.

"Makeup? Really?" He stepped a little closer. "I couldn't really tell, but...I like it. You look even better than you normally do, and you're always pretty."

Angie's expression cracked a little. The corners of her mouth edged upward. "I want to wear it to school. Tomorrow. The other girls do."

"I don't care about the other girls," he said. But just as Angie's face began to sag a little, he added, "Yes, you can wear it to school. It's very tasteful. Did Hope show you how to do that?"

Angie nodded, and a smile began to dawn on her face. "Yes. So I can wear it to school? Really?"

"Really," he agreed, smiling. "As long as you don't go all black lipstick and eye shadow on me."

Angie let out a happy whoop and dashed from the

room, calling over her shoulder that she was going to call Mary Lou right now.

Cash looked at Hope. "Mary Lou?"

"I have no idea. Maybe she's starting to make friends."

He stared upward. "God, I hope so."

"I hope you're not mad at me for doing this without clearing it with you."

He lowered his gaze to her face. "This is the first time I've heard that kind of laughter in this house for longer than I can remember. I'm grateful to you."

Hope nearly sagged with relief. The decision to do this had been an impulse, one she couldn't take back from the instant she had promised Angie a surprise. Nevertheless, once she had begun, she'd been constantly aware that she might be headed for trouble. She'd gone to school with plenty of girls whose parents had a problem with even the lightest dash of lipstick at this age.

She felt an urge to tell Cash that he'd handled it all beautifully, but withheld the words. It wasn't her place to offer opinions on his parenting. Instead, she cherished the glow he'd given her.

The first time he'd heard laughter in this house in forever? Now that was sad beyond description.

Pregnancy seemed to be making Hope tired. She retired early with a novel from Cash's library and curled up under warm covers to read by the bedside lamp. She drifted off quickly, before she had read more than a couple of pages.

But later, much later, she woke with a start and a sense of panic. She had trouble remembering where she was for a few seconds, and it took even longer for her heart rate to slow. What had she been dreaming?

As the lonely wind keened around the house, occasionally rattling her window, she huddled under the blankets, grateful the lamp was still on, trying to sort out reality from the nightmare. Dark figures had been chasing her, threatening her. She seemed to remember Scott's face in the mix somewhere. Well, she hardly needed to be a psychologist to figure that one out.

But she was safe now. Scott couldn't possibly want her anymore. She had fled him, in a way that left no doubt that she wasn't just a little "upset" about what he'd done. Much better for him to play the jilted fiancé who couldn't understand why she had left him than to drag her back to a place where she might just tell the truth. And even if he managed to deflect her claim of rape, it would haunt his entire future with questions.

So she was safe, she assured herself. If she'd been willing to settle down, stop making wild accusations and marry him that would have been different. But now... Now it was better for him if she just didn't come back.

All she had to do was keep her mouth shut and stay away—and she was perfectly willing to do that. She felt no particular desire for revenge. All she wanted to do was hide like a little mouse somewhere and bring up her child.

Maybe someday she'd even find a man who could truly love her and love her child. Was that too much to ask?

Now, however, she was wide-awake. Giving up finally, she unpacked her warmest robe and slippers and crept downstairs to make a cup of tea. There was too much going on inside her head, and none of it would leave her alone.

Scott. Well, he was starting to truly feel like the past.

But there was Angie and all her problems, and Cash, who seemed to be working harder than any man should. What's more, she clearly saw the flashes of pain and perplexity on his face when he looked at his daughter. Tonight had been the very first time she had felt a tenuous connection between them. Something to savor?

She hoped so. She hoped tomorrow wouldn't return to the icy wasteland she had seen between them in the past week.

Then there was her own reaction to Cash. He had begun to loom large on her radar. It honestly amazed her that she could feel attraction to a man after all that had happened, but she did. A strong and growing attraction.

His admission that he found her desirable had done nothing to frighten her, and little to help her banish her own awareness of him. Amazingly enough, she cherished his attraction to her deep inside.

Given what had happened to her with Scott, that seemed strange. She ought to feel repelled, and wondered why she didn't. Instead, knowing that he found her desirable had somehow made her feel better about herself. Maybe the rape and the way her family had treated her had left her feeling permanently soiled. Ruined. Unworthy.

She couldn't quite understand herself, but she knew what she was feeling. Cash had returned to her something that she seemed to have lost.

Of course, it wasn't enough to attract a man, or be attractive. She understood that. But a tiny healing had taken place, just a small one, in the gaping wound the past few months had inflicted on her. Cash didn't look at her and see a threat that needed to be dealt with. He saw a woman, a pregnant woman, and still found her appealing.

It was a good feeling.

She carried her tea into the living room, switched a lamp on low and curled up in a corner of the couch. The house felt chilly, so she tugged the afghan that hung over the back of the sofa and tucked it around herself.

The tea created a ball of warmth in her stomach, and she hoped she might doze off right here. It was a friendly room, welcoming with its well-used furnishings and bright colors. Very different from the house where she had grown up surrounded by the best and always kept up-to-date and in perfect shape. Her bedroom had been the only space that she had controlled, and even there, the minute she went out, one of the maids would swoop in to pick up after her. Privacy had been something she had barely been able to imagine.

Others, people she didn't know and wasn't supposed to talk to, had handled and touched everything she owned. The staff was supposed to be invisible, and they had been for years. Now, like Sleeping Beauty, she had wakened to a changed world, one that made her squirm a bit uncomfortably when she recalled that not only had she taken wealth for granted, she had taken people for granted. Live human beings.

"God," she whispered, and pulled the afghan closer around her shoulders. People like Hattie, who was being so helpful to her now. Except that in the Conroy household, the staff had not only been invisible, but they couldn't speak English. For the first time she wondered if that had been deliberate. Or maybe just cheaper.

At this point, little would have surprised her. She had seen the ugly side of her own parents, and if they had one ugly side they might have others.

What kind of illusion had she grown up in?

"Hope?"

Cash's voice startled her out of her reverie. She looked up to see him standing in the doorway, clad in jeans and a sweatshirt. His hair was tousled, his face unshaven and his boots had given way to socks.

"Are you okay?" he asked.

"I'm fine. I just couldn't sleep."

"So nothing's wrong?"

She shook her head. "I'm just remembering, and thinking that so much of my life looks different now. Like my view had been skewed."

"Then or now?"

"Then. Maybe."

He hesitated. "Want some company?"

"But you need your sleep!"

"I was awake, too. That's why I came down when I heard someone stirring. But I don't want to intrude. It's fine if you'd rather be alone."

She barely needed to think about it. She enjoyed Cash's companionship, possibly too much for her own good. "I'd like the company."

"Give me a couple. I need some coffee. You?"

"I'm having tea in the hopes it won't keep me awake."

He laughed. "I'm giving up. But don't hesitate to doze off if you feel like it."

He disappeared, leaving her to wonder if he might help derail her thoughts. It would be entirely too easy to fall into the blues if she spent too much time remembering. If she started wondering if her parents had ever loved her at all, or if they had seen her primarily as a social tool.

Cash returned soon with a mug of coffee. This time he sat on the other end of the couch from her, and not in his easy chair. That was fine by her. The way she was curled up, that made it easier for her to look at him, and she *did* enjoy looking at him.

"So what made you feel skewed?" he asked.

So much for avoiding that train of thought. She hesitated. "It's hard to explain. I think I grew up in a bubble."

"Meaning?"

"I was the center of my own little universe. Wealth makes that easy, I guess. Anyway, now that I've had to fight that bubble and run away from it, it's like I'm seeing it for the first time."

"Are you sorry it's gone?"

"Part of me is, but most of me is glad to be rid of it. Reality check time."

"But the bubble didn't protect you from everything," he said gently.

"Clearly." She felt her baby stir, as yet just faint movements, but very, very real to her. Beneath the afghan she placed a hand over her stomach.

"My mother crocheted that afghan," he remarked.

"Oh! Is it all right for me to use?"

"Of course." He smiled over his mug and took a sip. "She didn't make them to hang in a museum. I have one upstairs in my room, and I gave one to Angie. Mom liked to crochet, said it kept her hands busy in the evenings. If you want the truth, I think it kept her warm, too." He laughed quietly. "As soon as the temperature started to drop in the fall, she'd go buy plenty of yarn and start another afghan. I lost count of how many she gave away to her friends and for church fund-raisers. Anyway, by the time she started to complain that the house was draughty and she was cold, there'd be this partly finished afghan spread across her lap keeping her warm."

"Well, that's one way to do it." Hope smiled, imagining it. "You told me about your father's passing. What happened to your mother?"

"She liked to go on long rides when she could. One day she didn't come back, but her horse did. Unfortunately, it took us the better part of twenty-four hours to find her. She'd taken a fall, although we never knew for sure if something startled her mount and it threw her, or if she'd dismounted and then slipped. Either way..." He shrugged.

"Hence the rule about never riding alone."

He nodded.

"I'm sorry, Cash. How old were you?"

"Sixteen."

Hope could only shake her head, feeling sorrow for him. This man had never had an easy life, quite a contrast to her.

When he didn't speak again for a while, she tried to reach out to him with sympathy. "You've had a hard life."

He looked at her. "You think so? I don't."

"You don't?" That surprised her, especially as she had just been contrasting her own life of ease with his.

"Nope," he said firmly. "Hope, I'm pushing forty. Most men my age could tote up the same losses. Parents? Check. One divorce? Check. The normal course of life. If you ask me, you're the one who got the raw deal. Maybe you were in a bubble before, but it got ripped away from you in a horrible, terrible way. Now you're out here on your own trying to tame my daughter while carrying a child inside you. A single mom. No, that's a lot harder than my life, and it all came crashing down on you at once."

Her throat tightened a bit and she had to swallow

before she could speak. "You're a very generous man, Cash."

He shook his head. "Seems like I was right about one thing, though."

"What's that?"

"My daughter needed a companion closer to her own age. The sound of the two of you having such a good time did my soul good."

"You handled it well. We were both nervous about how you'd react."

"It's just a little makeup, not a crime." He flashed a grin. "I don't think she needs it, any more than you do, but…" He shrugged. "I get it. It's a girl thing."

"In some circles it's required. My mother got a professional to teach me how to apply it when I was fifteen. Every year or so, I got an update session."

"Really?" He sounded astonished.

"Really. Styles change, and as we age we need different amounts of makeup. Then you have to know what to wear according to the lighting conditions."

"Over-the-top?" he asked hesitantly.

"Not at the time. Now it looks like it to me. I'm actually enjoying not wearing any since I got here."

"Frankly, I approve. Nothing wrong with the way you looked when I interviewed you, but you have a fresh, very pretty face. It doesn't need enhancement."

She nearly blushed. "Cut it out, Cash."

His smile broadened. "Cut what out? Complimenting you?"

"You're embarrassing me."

"Okay. We'll talk about Angie, then. She seems to have settled a bit. At least she's not screaming at me."

At once Hope felt an internal jolt of nerves. She had promised Angie she wouldn't spy on her, but she felt it would help Cash ever so much to know the girl had been molested. The thing was, it was apt to put him through the roof, and she doubted he'd be able to conceal that he knew.

Which then would break the bridge she'd been trying to build with Angie. How could she keep his daughter's trust if she didn't keep her word? But she'd never imagined anything like that little bomb, and keeping it from Cash didn't seem right at all.

She sat there, unconsciously biting her lower lip, wondering how to handle it. She'd kept silent too long already, but on the other hand…maybe she'd come far enough with Angie to persuade her that her father needed to know about that man.

"Hope? What's worrying you?"

She felt like an open book, and she wasn't sure she liked it. "Nothing," she said finally. "Just thinking."

"About Angie?"

"Well, yes. It's true she's not screaming, at least not this week, but there's still plenty of ice there. I was just wondering how to get past it. It's not enough for her to like just me. She needs to trust you, too."

"I told you I wasn't hoping for a miracle." His tone had grown heavy. "I've just never been able to get close to her. I don't know why. Like I said, every time I saw her, I was a stranger all over again. And when her mother died, she lost everything. I get it. Maybe I'm all tangled up in it, because as far as she's concerned I took her away from everything she knew and brought her to the middle of nowhere."

"She just needs to settle in and make more friends," Hope said with more certainty than she felt. "I like it here. It's very different from the way I lived before, but I like it. It's peaceful and pretty, and I love being around horses again. Angie loves horses, too. She'll get over her sense of isolation."

"I hope so. I hear she's been taking care of her own mount. I appreciate that."

Hope almost giggled. "It's kind of hard for her not to when she sees me doing it. Maybe she'll discover how soothing it is, and how it creates a bond with her horse."

"I hope so. That's one of those things I don't tolerate. You have to care for your animals. Period."

Hope hesitated. "Have you thought about getting her a pet. A cat or dog? If she's willing to care for it, that is."

"It crossed my mind, but when she was refusing to care for her horse, I just couldn't see it. Maybe I'll consider it now."

Hope nodded, satisfied.

"Have you told her about your baby yet?"

"No." At once everything inside Hope tensed. "I know I have to, and soon, but it's so difficult. I'm trying to figure out how to approach it without telling her more than she needs to know."

"Like the fact you were raped by your fiancé?" He shook his head, his expression growing stern. "I'm all for protecting the innocence of childhood, but only to a point. There are some facts of life she needs to know for her own protection. I wouldn't spare her the truth about what happened to you. You don't need to give her details, but she needs to know that someone you trust isn't always safe."

Hope had to stifle the urge to tell him Angie wasn't as innocent as he thought, and that she was more aware of the facts of life than Cash suspected. "I'll try to talk to her tomorrow," she said.

"I know it's hard. I watched you struggle with telling me." He paused. "Hope? I've been wondering…

Don't you need some help dealing with this? A counselor? Something?"

"Eventually, maybe." She closed her eyes, turning inward. "Right now, I feel like I've dealt with it. Maybe that's just denial, but I had plenty of time to think about it all, four long months to be furious, sad, betrayed. I feel okay now that I'm away from it."

"How okay?" he asked. Then he slid down the couch until he was right beside her. "Nervous?"

Her eyes popped open and met his. Having him so close was awakening things in her that felt good, not bad.

"Hope?"

"I feel like I'm erasing Scott. He was one man, not all men. It's not like he was the only guy I ever dated. He's not my only point of comparison. And I didn't feel at all uneasy when you said you found me attractive. Quite the opposite."

"Really?" He held out his hand.

She knew what he was asking—was she really comfortable enough with what had happened to her that she could tolerate taking the hand of a man? Without hesitation, she freed one hand from the afghan and laid it in his. His palm was warm, work-roughened, his grip gentle as his fingers closed around hers.

He smiled, his eyes reflecting a heat that somehow didn't seem threatening. It seemed inviting.

"Good," he said.

The next thing she knew, he'd slipped his other arm around her and drew her against his hard, warm body. She caught her breath as an astonishing sense of hopeful expectation filled her. A wild sense that if he just made love to her, Scott would be forever banished. But that wouldn't be fair to him.

And evidently it wasn't what he wanted at all. He just held her in the midst of the quiet night, filling her with the belief that it all could get better.

All of it. She allowed her head to come to rest on his shoulder and closed her eyes. This was good and right. A long-unfamiliar warmth began to creep into her heart, along with yearnings she had thought she might never feel again. His shoulder was firm beneath her cheek, and the sound of his heartbeat comforting and strong. Like the man himself.

"Rest," he murmured. "Sleep if you can."

At first she didn't think that would be possible, as achy desire filled her, but perhaps a hug was exactly what she needed.

Because soon she drifted away into pleasant dreams about Cash, the most pleasant dreams she had had in months.

She slept safe in the circle of his arms.

Chapter Six

Cash couldn't explain it. For more than a decade now he'd felt no serious attraction for any woman. Since Sandy packed up and left, he'd concluded that he had nothing to offer, really, so why throw his heart into anything but his ranch?

He'd had a few flings with women who knew the score, but nothing that mattered. After a while he and they had parted ways amicably enough. He was no catch in any way that he could see. He spent too much time working, had little time for casual socializing, certainly no time to keep a wife happy, judging by Sandy's past remarks.

So what the hell was he thinking when it came to Hope? She said she was past Scott, but he wondered about that. Setting her aside for the moment, he had to wonder at himself. Nothing to offer a woman, but he was looking at Hope in a whole different way.

She wasn't a casual fling. She couldn't be. A meaningless romp would only wound her all over again. She was the marrying kind, especially since she had a child to think about. But despite his every effort, he felt pulled to her by hunger and something else, as if there was a rubber band between them trying to yank him closer.

Holding her last night had only made it worse. Just a hug, yet he felt as if the outlines of her soft body had been permanently tattooed on his. The fullness of her breast, the gentle curve of her hip, the weight of her head on his shoulder. Her womanly scent. Enough to drive any man mad, and he was no exception. One hug had turned him into a wildfire.

More than once he'd caught an expression in her face that suggested she was attracted to him, too. But that wasn't enough. Attraction would never be enough, and she was probably still more of a wreck than she realized.

He couldn't offer her healing. He was no counselor, and besides, he just plain had nothing to offer. He had a troublesome daughter and a ranch that consumed him, and that would never satisfy a woman.

What's more, she was used to a life so different from his it was almost beyond his imagining. Men who could take her out for fancy dinners and buy her roses. A family that probably thought nothing of taking European holidays and long skiing vacations at places he could never afford.

So what if she said she liked it here. Soon enough she'd realize there was little to be found here at all.

So he had to be smart and not cross any lines. For both their sakes.

So what the hell had he been doing last night, holding her while she fell asleep against him? Being brotherly? Hah! He knew himself better than that.

He looked at her and thought she might need some professional help. Looking at himself, he realized he might need the same thing. All this time and he evidently still hadn't recovered from the blow Sandy had dealt him.

If there was anything to recover from. Hell, she'd taught him a lesson, and he'd thought he had learned it. Maybe not.

For some reason in the past week, old dreams had been surfacing, dreams of family and home, and a woman to come home to every night. It was an illusion, one he could never bring to reality, but he had begun enjoying coming home after working with the cattle to find lights on, dinner in the oven and a smiling woman waiting for him. It was just a step away from pretending they were a happy family.

And the laughter last night had almost put a seal on it. A man could work his heart out for that warmth and laughter, that welcome.

That was his problem, wasn't it? Working his heart out. Loving the ranch more than anything else, according to Sandy. More than her.

Those remarks had been scalding him for over a decade now. It was a barrier he couldn't find a way to cross. If a woman couldn't see it, how could you explain to her that working that hard was a mark of his devotion to his family? What was he supposed to do? Let everything go slowly to ruin, leaving them homeless and hungry?

It was a question he'd never been able to answer. Certainly not in a way Sandy had understood. Now he was having these vague thoughts about Hope, a woman who was used to being treated like a princess?

Hell, he really *did* need his head examined. Wanting her wasn't enough. It would never answer the questions.

He mounted up and rode over to the chutes where he and his three men were going to check out the rest of the cattle, count how many were pregnant.

The work was never done.

Hope waited nervously for Angie to come home. She wanted to hear about the makeup experience today, maybe learn something about who Mary Lou was, and finally, like it or not, she was going to have to address her pregnancy.

God, she wasn't looking forward to this, but she couldn't let it go any longer. The looser clothes might not be a giveaway, though soon her baby bump would really show. Angie would have every right to feel Hope had been keeping important secrets, and given the girl's fragile state, she'd probably find it cause to distrust even more. Or direct her anger at Hope.

Her mind kept wandering back to falling asleep in Cash's arms last night. It had been innocent enough on the face of it, but it filled her with a glow and had ignited a small sense of future possibilities in her. Cash didn't find her repugnant because she had been raped. He wasn't repelled by her pregnancy. Instead, he had welcomed her into his embrace, making her feel safe. Better, he made her feel okay, something she had not felt since the rape.

Months of hearing that she was a liar, an ingrate, a stupid child and even worse had seriously chipped away at her self-image. She had been told more than once that if Scott had had sex with her, it was *her* fault. She must have invited it. She must have teased him. She must have done *something* bad. It was all on her.

There were times when she had even questioned her own sanity, and all that saved her was the reality of the child growing in her. She hadn't imagined that. And no matter how many times she examined her actions that night, she couldn't see what she might have done that made Scott think she wanted to be taken over her own protests. No meant no, didn't it?

Apparently not in Scott's world. At times when she forced herself to remember, she had the distinct impression that he had taken her struggles and her telling him to stop as part of a game, a challenge of some type. Then when it was over and she was sobbing he told her to grow up—she had nothing to cry about because they were going to get married soon. As if a piece of paper could bandage that wound.

She stifled a sigh and glanced at the clock. Any minute now. Start cheerfully, she cautioned herself. Keep the conversation to school, makeup, Mary Lou while Angie got her snack. Then…well… She couldn't help but feel she might be going to the executioner. If all of this was hard to explain to herself, how much harder to share it with a thirteen-year-old.

At last she heard the front door open. Her heart picked up pace and it was suddenly difficult to keep her face smooth. She heard the door close, the backpack bang as it was dropped at the foot of the stairs. Then she heard something for the very first time: Angie called her name.

"Hope?"

"I'm in the kitchen."

Angie's step was quick and light, and when she appeared in the kitchen, she was grinning. "Everybody liked my makeup!"

"Wonderful." Hope smiled broadly. "I'm so happy for you."

"Only the girls noticed it, of course, but that was the plan, right?"

"Well, only a girl would notice it when you've done it so tastefully."

"Thank you! I had a great day today. Since Mary Lou started talking with me last week, some of the other girls have started to pay attention to me. Today I felt like I had a crowd again." She opened the fridge and pulled out some milk, filling a glass then grabbing some cookies from the cookie jar. Moments later, she was sitting at the table with Hope.

"You've been missing your friends, haven't you?"

Angie nodded. "I had two really close friends in Arizona, and I miss them. But now I think I can make new ones."

"I'm sure you can."

"Anyway, some of them asked me if you'd give them lessons on makeup, too. Maybe Dad will let some of them come over on Saturday?"

"We'll have to ask. I can't answer for him."

Angie's face darkened a bit, then brightened again. "He'll say yes," she said decisively.

Hope laughed lightly, refusing to say anything because it wasn't her place. She suspected Angie was right, though.

"So will you do it?" Angie asked. "Show them?"

"Sure. But ask them to bring their own makeup, and try to match their skin tone as closely as they can."

"I was telling them all about that today," Angie said proudly. Then she hesitated. "I just said you had a lot of training in makeup. I didn't say you're my nanny."

"I don't exactly feel like a nanny. Is that how you think of me?"

Angie shook her head quickly. A crumb went flying from the corner of her mouth. "No. You don't feel like that. More like...an older friend?"

Hope didn't know how ready she was to be referred to as older, but regardless, this was a huge step. And she was still looking for an entrée to bring up her pregnancy. Then she had a thought.

"Angie, before you invite your friends over, there's something you need to know about me. I don't want to cause you any trouble."

Angie put her cookie down, swallowed some milk and grabbed a paper napkin from the basket on the table to wipe her mouth. "You mean that you're pregnant? I wondered if you'd tell me."

Hope's jaw dropped open. "How did you know?"

"One of the girls at school said you were buying maternity clothes yesterday. Her mother works at Freitag's. Everyone thinks my dad is the father, but I told them he can't be because you only got here a week ago. Even kids my age can count."

Hope sat back, simply staring in disbelief. "It got around that fast?"

"I'm learning that things get around really fast in this place. Like lightning. I guess cuz all people have to talk about is other people."

"Well." Flummoxed, Hope tried to absorb this. Although why she should feel surprised she didn't know. Things had got around fast in her old circles. Not around town, but within her circles.

"It's okay," Angie said. "You aren't the first single mom around here. What happened?"

Another reason to hesitate. *I was raped* sounded so bald. "You know what happened to you?"

"Almost happened," Angie corrected. "Yeah?"

"Like that. Only worse. And he was my fiancé."

Angie lost all interest in her snack, looking at her intently. "Did you call the cops?"

"I couldn't."

"Why not? My mom didn't hesitate." Then, "Oh. I get what you meant when you said I was lucky my mother believed me. But you're older!"

"Circumstances…" Hope trailed off. "It's hard to explain."

"Try me. I want to know."

But how could you explain a world where appearances were everything, and a man's political career mattered more than his actions? If she hadn't lived through it, she wouldn't have believed it. Angie was still waiting, however, and there didn't seem to be any way out of it.

"My fiancé was an important man. Nobody believed me, not even my parents. They wanted to force me to marry him, anyway, and if I didn't they insisted I have an abortion. So…"

Angie's eyes widened. "So you ran away?"

"Yes, I did. After nearly four months of being badgered and called a liar, I couldn't take it anymore and I ran."

"Wow," Angie said quietly. For several minutes, the only sound in the kitchen was the hum of the refrigerator. "That's awful, Hope. I'm sorry. I thought about running away a few times, but where could I go?"

"I was past caring where I went. I had to save myself and my baby. Landing here was lucky for me."

"Lucky? Looking after the imp from hell?"

Hope was horrified. "Who called you that?"

"Nobody." Angie gave a sheepish grin. "I half expected Dad to get around to it, the way I was acting. He never did. He just looked worried and upset."

"He is worried about you. You've been through a terrible time. You really ought to talk to him. He knows you hated losing everything and having to come here to what he called the middle of nowhere. He gets it, Angie."

Angie looked down at her plate, pushing cookie crumbs around with her finger. "He's okay. I mean, I think I would have thrown myself out months ago. Funny how having you here made me see how awful I was acting. I still don't…"

"Don't what?" Hope finally prodded.

"I don't feel close to him. I mean, he's never here, really. He's working all the time, just like my mom said. She said the ranch mattered more to him than her or me."

"I'm not sure that's true. This place needs a lot of work. He's trying to pay bills and buy food and all that."

"I know. My brain knows. But sometimes I wonder if he'd even notice if I disappeared."

"Oh, Angie, I know he would. I'm here only because he's so worried about you. And he gave me the job because he said you didn't need another parent, you needed someone closer to your age so maybe we could relate. That's hardly a sign of not caring."

"I guess." Angie had started to look uncomfortable. "I guess I should give him a chance, huh?"

"You could try. It's not too late to have a relationship. And I know he cares about you. He's said it often enough."

"I'll think about it." That seemed to close the subject. "So you'll give lessons to my friends?"

"I'd be happy to."

"Awesome!" Angie popped up, drained her milk glass and skipped out, saying, "Lots of homework."

Hope watched her go with mixed feelings. On the one hand, they'd had a pretty good conversation, and Angie had accepted the news of Hope's pregnancy pretty well. On the other, she was still left keeping a secret about Angie's past. The longer this went on, the worse she felt about not telling Cash, but she couldn't tell him about the molestation without discussing it first with Angie. It could wind up blowing up everything they'd been building.

She was sure, however, that Cash would want to know about something so important. It would help him understand his daughter, and he didn't seem like the kind of man who wanted important information kept from him.

But Hope didn't even know how long ago this had happened to Angie. She'd mentioned it, which meant it was important in her mind, but what could Cash do about it now? Nothing. Hope still felt he needed to know. It was part of the anger and distrust that brewed in the girl. For all Hope knew, in some way Angie held Cash responsible for not being there to protect her. She might not be a practicing psychologist, but she'd done enough course work to have an idea of the kinds of games a mind could play.

Maybe Angie even believed that Cash knew about it and wondered why he hadn't come racing to her side.

God, that was an awful possibility to contemplate.

It was possible, of course, that Cash had heard about it, that Sandy had let him know. But it didn't seem like Cash to ignore such a thing. He'd been pretty straightforward and clear-sighted about the problems Angie was dealing with. Surely he wouldn't have failed to tell her Angie had been molested, certainly not when he must know that Hope of all people would understand the fallout from that.

She put her head in her hand, trying to figure out what to do and when. Go up now and invade the girl in her room? Wait for another opportune time? Or just flat out tell Cash and let the chips fall?

She felt her youth and inexperience acutely right then. Her bubble hadn't prepared her for questions like these. But honestly, it hadn't prepared her for raising her own child, either.

God, she had so much to figure out.

Cash approved the makeup party without hesitation, and even suggested that if Angie wanted, she could invite her friends to stay the night. "Movies and popcorn," he said. "And lots of noise, I imagine."

For once Angie giggled at something he said, but then dashed off, probably to make phone calls.

They sat at the table, Cash with a half smile on his face. Angie hadn't finished her dinner, but neither had they.

"Wow," he said finally. "Miracles do happen." Then he looked at Hope. "I don't know how much you had to do with this, but thank you. Things have been changing since you arrived. And now that you're here, a pajama party can be properly chaperoned. I didn't want to suggest it before when it was just me. I mean, everyone around here knows me, but that's no guarantee they'd be comfortable letting their daughters stay over with me being the only adult in the house."

"They probably would," Hope said, even though she had no way of knowing. "I think it's helping that Angie started to make a friend last week. Then some of the other girls started talking to her."

"Makeup appears to have had a lot to do with that. Well, we'll see what other parents think about their girls coming over here to have a makeup party. Maybe I shouldn't have suggested an overnighter. What if no one wants to come?"

Good question, thought Hope. She couldn't imagine it being the case, but that didn't mean it wouldn't happen. The parents might know Cash, but they didn't know Angie. Her hands tightened as she thought of Angie's possible disappointment. The little bit of progress they'd made could be seriously set back.

"Fits and starts," Cash murmured, as if his thoughts were running along the same lines. "I'm sure we're not out of the woods yet, but this is a positive sign."

Hope nodded, and once again her thoughts trailed guiltily to the secret she was keeping from him. It was Angie's secret, of course, not hers to share, but she felt guilty, anyway, and wondered why. Cash might need to know so he could respond better to Angie, but on the other hand, how could she be sure it would make any difference?

Then another thought occurred to her. "You know, if the girls don't come it could be because of me. I hope Angie knows that. Maybe I should warn her."

"What would you have to do with it?"

"Angie said earlier that word had gotten around that I'm pregnant. Some parents might not want their daughters hanging with a single mom."

"I didn't think of that." His face darkened. "Hell, I hope my neighbors are better people than that."

"It's not about the kind of people they are, it's about

being concerned about the influences their daughters are exposed to. They don't know me."

He leaned forward a bit, his eyes narrowing. "It won't be about you. It'll be their judgment of me. I invited you into my home to take care of my daughter. If they think I'd expose Angie to a bad influence, it won't be about you."

He pushed away from the table. "I'll help with the dishes."

"Don't you have work to do?"

"Always."

"Then go do it. I've got this." She watched him disappear down the hall with a muttered thanks, and then started clearing the table. How had such a simple thing become so complicated?

Because life was never simple, answered a voice in her head. Time to learn that, too.

Angie caught Hope at the top of the stairs later as she was coming up to read and get ready for bed. Her eyes sparkled, a good sight, but she looked a little doubtful, as well.

"Hope, can you talk?"

"Sure." She followed Angie into her bedroom. It was a cheerful space, full of bright colors, stuffed animals and a few things that looked like Angie's keepsakes, such as a teddy bear that looked both worn and old.

Angie closed the door and sat on the edge of her bed. "The girls are going to ask their parents."

"Good." Hope settled into a Boston rocker in the corner. "Any problems?"

"I don't know." Angie bit her lip. "Hope, what if they say no?"

"Some of them might have other things to do. How many did you invite?"

"Five. The ones who talked to me most today."

Hope nodded. Tension was building in her again, and it seemed to reach her baby. She felt the familiar flutters and placed her hand over her stomach. "If they can't come, don't take it personally."

"*All* of them? That would be personal."

Hope had seen Angie angry, happy and most places in between over the past ten days, but this was the first time she had seen the girl looking ready to crumble. She wished she dared cross the room and give her a hug, but so far she hadn't been invited into that kind of contact. "We don't know what they're going to say yet. Regardless, if they don't come it'll probably be about me, not you."

"Why would it be about you?" Then Angie's face changed. "Oh."

"Exactly. You said everyone knows I'm pregnant. The parents could wonder if I'm a bad influence."

Now Angie looked angry. "If they think that, they don't know my dad."

Hope felt a brief flicker of amusement. Amazing how closely Angie's thoughts ran to her dad's. She might have pointed that out under different circumstances.

"Well, we don't know yet," she finally said, trying to be practical. "Let's not borrow trouble."

Angie curled her legs under her and reached for a throw pillow to hug. "They were nice to me today. *They* were the ones who wanted you to teach them how to do makeup."

"That was your friends, though, not their parents."

"I know. Parents can be so stupid sometimes."

"Tell me about it."

Angie peered at her. "Hope? What was it like being rich?"

Hope hesitated. "It's hard to explain. Plus, my experience wouldn't be everyone's."

"Tell me, anyway," Angie insisted. "Did you have everything you wanted? Travel a lot?"

Hope looked down. "I never wanted for things. I had plenty of *things*. And yes, we traveled a lot. Skiing in Aspen or Europe, yachting with friends, shopping trips to New York and Paris. A lot of it was like a storybook."

"That must have been nice."

Hope struggled, trying to put her new understanding into words. "It had its problems, too."

"Like being raped and not being believed?"

"Not being really loved."

Angie drew a sharp breath. "My mom loved me."

"Yes, she did. And so does your dad. They cared about you. Me, I was…" Again she paused.

"Hope?" Angie pressed her impatiently.

Hope didn't want to discuss this at all. She was still having trouble framing this whole mess and her changing worldview. She'd had a shocking awakening and still couldn't fully deal with it. She didn't want to dash a young girl's illusions, but she didn't want to create any, either. On the horns of a dilemma, she began rocking, hoping that Angie could be just a little more patient. There had to be a way to address this.

And maybe explaining it to Angie would help her, too.

"Imagine," she said finally, "this big, beautiful soap bubble floating along. It blows this way and that in the wind, and it's full of rainbow colors. Then imagine a woman, a girl, inside it. The world outside can't touch her, and she can't touch it. She just lives in her rainbow bubble."

She stole a glance at Angie and saw the girl nod, her brow knitting.

"So anyway, the girl in the bubble thinks everything is perfect, she goes where the wind tells her, just floating along. She gets pushed toward a marriage and everything seems great. It's what she was raised to do. A prominent prince, a bright future, everything according to the plan."

"And then?"

"And then the bubble pops. The rainbows are gone, reality is suddenly close and real, and she's not really prepared for it. Her bubble was an illusion, and everything was taken from her. Even the people she thought loved her turn out to have been just a rainbow in a bubble."

Angie drew a long breath. Then she asked a question that drove straight to the heart and didn't really have an adequate answer. "So what's real?"

Hope looked down at her hand cradling her stomach. "This baby. I'd say love, but apparently I never really had much of that to begin with. Anyway, you're real, your dad is real, this ranch is real and I've still got a lot to learn."

"Love," Angie repeated. "Even that goes away."

Hope looked up instantly. "Your mom didn't choose to leave you."

"No, but your parents did."

"Well, not exactly."

"Yes, exactly." Angie scowled. "You had to run away, you said. To protect yourself from them. That's not love."

"Then tell me what love is, Angie."

"Me? I'm just a kid. I just know Mom loved me. Enough to throw out her boyfriend and go to court to keep him away from me."

"That's love all right."

"I don't know about my dad, though. He *had* to take me."

Hope stood up, unexpected anger surging in her as she reacted to an attitude that had been bothering her since her first day here. She had to struggle to keep her voice calm. "Here's something for you to consider. He *did not* have to take you. He could have signed you over to foster care. Instead, he brought you here, and he's been putting up with your temper for months now. I get your anger. So does he, actually. But he did not have to take you in."

Leaving Angie gaping, Hope walked out, closing the door quietly behind her.

What had brought that on? Talking about bubbles? Thinking that maybe Angie was creating one for herself, a dark one that wasn't fair to Cash?

Oh, God, maybe she had just done a terrible thing. Maybe she had just shattered every gain they'd made. Suddenly frightened by her own behavior, she hurried downstairs to look for Cash. He needed to know what she had just said, even if it meant he threw her out.

She had no business talking to Angie that way. No business at all.

Cash was on the phone. He'd just started shutting down his computer for the night and was laughing with a parent of one of the girls Angie had invited over on Saturday. Yes, the invitation had his approval. Yes, Angie's nanny would be there. Yes, it was all about popcorn, movies and makeup. It was the fifth call and, he hoped, the last. The problems he had feared weren't arising, and tomorrow Angie would hear from all the friends she had invited. Everyone would come.

He hung up, relieved, and made the last selection to shut down the computer. Then he heard the hurried steps on the stairs and swiveled around to see Hope.

"What's wrong?" he asked instantly. A dozen awful possibilities flitted instantly across his mind. From her drained, pinched look it was clear that something bad had happened. "Are you okay?"

"That's the question, isn't it?"

He stood up, his heart accelerating. "Do you need a doctor?"

"Nothing like that. No, I said something to Angie that I probably shouldn't have said, and now I'm worried I messed everything up."

He didn't know whether to relax or get uptight. Clearly Hope was worried, but what could she have said that was so awful? After ten days, he thought he had a measure of her, and it was a good one. She was actually a very soothing presence to have around, except when he was reacting to her sexually. But that wasn't her fault. And at least it wasn't a problem right now, with her looking so upset.

"Time for tea?" he asked.

"I don't know. Maybe it's time for me to pack."

That really jolted him. He liked having her here. Maybe it was all imaginary, but he was starting to feel as if he had a family of sorts. "Let's not jump fences until we need to," he said. "Get comfortable. I'll get you some tea and we'll talk."

And damned if he could imagine what she could have said to Angie that would make him want to throw Hope out. He returned with coffee and tea as quickly as he could, anxious to get to the root of all this.

She'd remained in his office, choosing to sit on the wooden chair rather than seek the more comfortable living room. She looked as if she expected to be punished. His chest tightened at the sight.

God, what she must have been through with her family to be reacting to him this way. He wished he knew how to make her feel easier, but he couldn't say a word until he knew what was going on. He handed her the tea, then closed the door for privacy. Taking his desk chair, holding his own mug in both his hands, he said, "Well?"

"I got mad at Angie," she said stiffly, as if every nerve in her was so coiled that even speaking was difficult.

"You? Angry?" He could have laughed.

"This isn't a joke, Cash."

"I can see that. But you're always so restrained I was beginning to wonder if your upbringing had crushed every unpleasant feeling out of you."

"Apparently not."

"Nice to know you can be human. So what happened?"

"Of course I'm human, and I just proved it. God, what are you thinking?"

"Only that you're so ladylike most of the time you could be a plastic doll. Let it rip."

She gaped at him. "That wasn't kind."

"No, but it's true. Try being a little less perfect. Anyway, what are you worrying about?"

"I got mad at Angie, like I said. She made some remark about how you'd *had* to take her in. I don't know what got into me, but I didn't like that. I told her in no uncertain terms that you didn't have to take her, that you could have signed her over to foster care and she needed to think about that when she was judging you."

"I see." And he *did* see. Ripples spreading out. So Angie thought he'd had no choice but to take her and was thinking she was here only out of his sense of duty. Well, he did feel a duty, but it went beyond that. Poor as their relationship had been all these years, he cared about the child. He nurtured an abiding love for her even if she drove him nuts and he couldn't figure out what the hell was wrong between them.

He put his cup down and stood. "Time for me to have some words with my daughter."

"But Cash…"

"But what? What you said was true. Maybe she'll believe it from me. I should have said it a long time ago, anyway."

He opened the door and marched up the stairs. He heard Hope's light step behind him, but he didn't care if she listened to what he had to say. She hung back in the hallway, though, as he rapped on Angie's door.

"Go away. I'm sleeping."

"In a minute," Cash said. He opened the door and stepped one pace into a nearly dark room.

"Dad…"

"Listen to me. Just listen. Hope's upset because she told you that I could have put you in foster care. Well, I could have, but I didn't. I think it's time you knew why."

Angie didn't answer immediately, but she did eventually reach over to turn on the little lamp beside her bed. "So tell me," she said truculently.

"It's simple. When you were born I held you in my arms. I can still remember looking down into your pinched little face, hearing your very first cries. In that instant I loved you more than anything on earth. I would have died for you."

"Yeah, right."

"Leave your commentary out of this. Your mother never understood, and I guess she made the same complaints to you. Everything I did from that moment on was for you and her. When my dad got sick, I had to take over the whole job of running this place. I was working all the time, and I know your mother didn't like it. It wasn't fun. Hell, *I* didn't like it. But I did it because I had to. Because I had a little girl to take care of. Because I had to make sure you had food and a roof and clothes. I never did it for *me*, Angie. I did it for your mom and mostly for you. Because I loved you."

"Why did you let us go, then?"

"Was I going to keep you prisoners? Your mom hated it here and she took you away. You probably hardly remember my visits. You certainly don't remember all the money I sent so you both could live well. I sent more than I was required to because I never wanted you to do without. But that meant I had to work. I've never been a rich man, and hanging on to this place hasn't been easy, but it's the only work I know. It's the only way I can take care of you. I don't resent that, because I love you."

Angie remained silent.

"I'm sorry I'm not around more," Cash finished finally. "There's just so much of me, and so many hours in a day. But when you start to think I'm avoiding you, I want you to know that's the last thing I want to do. I love you. I guess only you can decide whether to believe it."

Then he stepped back out and closed the door. Turning, he saw Hope standing at the top of the stairs, tears running down her cheeks. A shaky whisper escaped her.

"Angie doesn't know how lucky she is." Then Hope

fled to her own room, leaving Cash to stare at closed doors and wonder how the hell he could fix everyone's life, including his own.

Because trying to do the right thing had apparently busted everything all to hell.

Chapter Seven

Ice settled again over the Cashford household. Angie's withdrawal tore at Hope, and the only positive omen she could find was that Angie still intended to have her friends over on Saturday.

Angie barely spoke at all, and once she told Hope, "You said you wouldn't spy on me."

"I didn't!"

"You told my dad what I said."

"I told your dad what *I* said and not one word more." But Angie was already heading out the door for school.

Tension plagued Hope. She thought she'd left a lot of that behind when she'd fled her family, but she was rapidly discovering that it seemed to be part of any family. Things got bad sometimes. All she could do was hope this would pass.

She felt guilty, though. Really, she'd had no business saying anything to Angie about why her father had chosen to bring her here. It wasn't her place, she didn't really know if she was right when she spoke and it didn't make her feel any better that Cash had confirmed it. Especially since he had done so by confronting his daughter, which might have made everything worse for the two of them.

The fact was, she acknowledged glumly, her charmed upbringing hadn't done much to prepare her for the real world. Cash was right about one thing: she'd been raised to be ladylike at all times. Smiling, charming, courteous, always pleasant. No outbursts of any kind. Maybe she *was* little better than a plastic wind-up doll. Her first step out of the mold and she had brought back the Ice Age to this house.

God, she knew better than that. Never speak unless you had something nice to say. Never get angry. Never erupt. For heaven's sake, never speak an unpleasant truth.

She nearly sickened herself, although it was hard to sort out whether she felt sicker about the kind of person she'd been raised to become, or about her less-than-ladylike behavior with Angie. Either way, she clearly wasn't suited to helping any thirteen-year-old grow up. It seemed all she could do was create new problems because she didn't know how to deal.

Friday afternoon, Angie called from school to say she would spend the night at Mary Lou's. Cash was out in the pastures, beyond reach, so Hope took her courage in her hands and asked for Mary Lou's mother's number to make sure it was all okay.

"I don't lie," Angie said sharply.

"I didn't say you did," Hope answered, staying calm. "But I also remember a time when I made a plan with a friend and we neglected to tell anyone where we were going to be. The police were out looking for us when we didn't come home. I didn't know I'd done anything wrong until then."

Angie sighed audibly, but gave her the phone number. Mary Lou's mother was both warm and friendly on the phone and admitted she'd heard of the girls' plan only a few minutes before and had instructed Angie to clear it. "I think they got all excited and forgot they needed to talk to anyone." She laughed. "But that's fine. The more the merrier. You still want them there at three tomorrow?"

That settled, Hope set about pulling out the night's dinner. She still hadn't tried her hand at solo cooking, but Hattie had promised to let her try next week.

If she was still here next week. She needed to talk to Cash, explain how inadequate she felt, and why she wasn't sure she was the best choice for this job. It wouldn't be easy to put her morass of feelings into some kind of comprehensible framework, though. She wasn't sure she grasped it herself.

All she knew was that she had helped precipitate a problem, and she feared she might do more harm.

When Cash at last returned for dinner, he looked tired and chilled. It didn't seem like a good time to broach her concerns, so Hope simply heated the casseroles while he went to shower and change.

She discovered she liked the way he smelled when he came in from working with his cattle. Some people might have found the odor unpleasant, but she found it rich and earthy. She liked it almost as much as she liked the way he smelled right after his shower.

He returned downstairs in his uniform of jeans and a sweatshirt, boots once again giving way to stocking feet.

"Where's Angie?" he asked as he looked at the table set for two.

"She's staying with Mary Lou tonight. I hope it's all right that I said yes. I talked with Mary Lou's mother."

"The Suttons? Good people. That's fine. And frankly I wouldn't mind a little global warming in this house."

Hope's heart and stomach sank simultaneously. She knew he must have been feeling Angie's withdrawal as well, but she had hoped it hadn't been as obvious to him. Apparently he was more aware than one would think, given how much he worked.

She hurried to get him a cup of the hot coffee she had made fresh for him, and put it in front of him as he sat at the table.

"You don't have to wait on me," he said a bit sharply.

"I'm not, really." Although she was, she supposed. "Sorry."

"Don't be sorry. Sit with me."

So she pulled out a chair across from him and joined him. For some reason, cold seemed to be sinking into her very bones. Everything was wrong, and she couldn't escape the feeling it was her fault.

"Cash?"

He cocked his head to one side and studied her. "You look like a frightened deer. Sorry I snapped. I had a cow with a twisted stomach today. The vet had to come out and stitch it into place."

The things she didn't know. "How can their stomachs twist?"

He shrugged. "Big stomachs. Four of them, and the very last one just kind of floats inside them. Lots of gas from grazing. Sometimes things bollix up."

"Will she be okay?"

"Probably. So will her calf. I was afraid she'd lose it." He sighed. "Sorry I was grumpy."

"You have a right. I messed things up, didn't I?"

His expression slowly changed from weary to astonished. "How the hell did you mess things up?"

"Well…" She hesitated. "I should never have confronted Angie. Apparently I made everything worse."

He snorted. "Worse? You really have no idea what I've been dealing with. I guess you only got a small glimpse. Regardless, I've been thinking it was time to put my foot down about something. I'm getting damn sick of tiptoeing around a thirteen-year-old like some kind of time bomb."

"She has been through a rough time," Hope said, having nothing else to offer.

"I know she has. I'm not a fool. But sooner or later she has to start behaving, and I'm wondering if I've been indulging her for too long. Grief and anger are no excuse to trample people. There are other ways of expression."

He paused, then rose to refill his mug. When he returned to the table, he remained silent for a couple of minutes, then spoke again. "I guess I've been letting her get away with too much because I felt guilty. I'm not sure what I'm guilty of, though. I didn't leave her and her mother—they left me. I didn't kill her mom. I didn't ignore her all these years—she pretty much ignored me. I'm running out of excuses here. I kept thinking she would start to settle in and make friends and it wouldn't seem so bad to her. Now she's making friends and we get more of this behavior."

"That's my fault," Hope hastened to say. "I should never have gotten angry like that, or told her that you didn't have to take her in."

"Why not? It's true. It's time she faced some truth. Anyway, you're human, too. Time for her to recognize that other people have feelings."

"But…" Hope bit her lower lip. "I'm not sure I'm good enough to do this, Cash. I've been thinking… things were getting better before I got angry. I put my foot in it and made them worse."

He arched a brow. "Don't tell me you actually thought we had a miraculous cure going here. I told you, fits and starts. She's not going to change overnight. Her anger isn't going to vanish in a snap. It's going to take time. And while I'm on the subject of you, I didn't ask you to be a miracle worker. I wanted to give her someone she could connect with, at least a little, who could help keep an eye on her. You were and are doing just fine. I don't hold you responsible for the current deep freeze. We had a January thaw. It passed. Now we're back to status quo." Then he smiled faintly. "Well, not quite status quo. I bet she didn't cancel the makeup party for tomorrow."

"Not yet."

"And she won't. But I am going to demand she treat you, me and everyone else in this house with common courtesy. She ought to be able to manage that much."

He was so kind, Hope thought again. Generous. But she still needed to address her basic issue. "I'm not sure I'm adequate for this," she said. "And no matter what you say, I feel like I put my foot in it and made things worse. What if I do that again?"

"We'll all do that from time to time. Why should Angie be the only one with a temper?" He peered at her. "What happened to your self-confidence?"

"What?" The question startled her.

He drummed his fingers on the table, gaze growing

distant. "I bet you were quite comfortable and confident in your old life."

"I think so." Her heart began to race nervously. Where was he going with this?

"Right now," he said slowly, "you feel like a fish out of water, don't you?"

She nodded slowly. "I guess so."

He smiled wryly. "Welcome to the club. The first Angie for both of us."

A surprised laugh escaped her.

"Exactly," he said. "We're both on a learning curve here. Just trust your instincts. And while you're at it, quit trying to be the model young woman I think your parents wanted you to be. Here you can get dirty and grubby and speak your mind. In fact, I'd appreciate it if you would. Smooth, smiling faces make me nervous."

"You? Nervous? I make you nervous?"

"You betcha," he said firmly. "I'm always wondering what you're not saying. Do me a favor, and say it. I like to know where I stand."

She almost laughed again, but then a startling truth hit home. "I'm not even sure I can think most of those thoughts."

"Straitjacketed, huh? I'm not surprised. Groomed like a prize filly, you said. Perfect training to be someone's perfect wife, I bet."

She nodded, hating the sound of it. A wild mixture of emotions was exploding in her, impossible to sort out anything except that she was afraid. She just wasn't sure what she was afraid of. "I only realized that just recently."

"Well, we need to rub some of that off on Angie, and some of Angie off on you." But there was a twinkle in his eye. "Look, you had the gumption to stand up to your family and leave home. So every time you start to doubt yourself, I suggest you remember that. You have more than enough strength. You just need to believe it."

"Easier said than done. I just don't know how to deal with someone Angie's age. Or someone who is going through what she is. I'm honestly afraid I'm going to mess up big-time." There it was, she thought. Fear of failure. That had been drilled into her for years. Fear of failure and now fear she would lose the home she had found here, yet feeling bound to give this man an out. God, couldn't she just stop running from everything?

"I doubt it." He paused. "You said you studied psychology."

"I learned in a classroom. That's different from knowing what to do with it."

His eyes narrowed a bit. "Are you trying to quit on me?"

"I'm trying to give you the freedom to fire me without guilt."

He surprised her with a hearty laugh. She gaped at him.

"You're not going to get out of this that easily," he told her. "Hah! If you don't want to quit, there's nothing to discuss. Like I said, I wasn't expecting miracles. It's going to take time to sort that girl out. I've been making an effort for months now, but I'm beginning to think I was too easy on her. Making too many excuses. If you think you caused fireworks, just wait until you see what happens when I start making demands of her. In the meantime, we have a night when she isn't around to stress either of us, so let's have dinner and figure out something entertaining to do. And for heaven's sake, will you please start speaking your mind? Between Angie who has no brakes on her mouth, and you, who seem to have nothing but brakes, I could go nuts."

Hope felt her face sag. "I'm really sorry."

"I'm not. It's like the contrast between hot and cold. Always changing. At least I'm not bored."

The oven timer dinged, but before she could take care of it, he rose and went to the oven. She didn't like being compared to cold, but she supposed there was some truth in it. Angie met everything with open passion, for good or ill. Hope, by complete contrast, met everything as if she were walking on eggshells. Trying to be perfect.

But the air felt clearer to Hope now. It *was* pleasant having dinner without a glowering Angie. And yet, she still wasn't sure the issue was settled. No matter how she looked at it, she knew she wasn't experienced in any useful way when it came to Angie, and it was little help that Cash was apparently feeling the same way. But the more she thought about it, the more she became certain that he was right: maybe he'd been too easy on her because of what she'd been through. Maybe Hope was doing the same thing, trying to keep things smoothed over.

After all, that's how she had been raised. Keep everything on an even keel. Short of unavoidable catastrophe, stay calm and pleasant.

"Donna Reed," she said suddenly.

They had moved to the living room with after-dinner coffee and tea. She sat on her end of the couch, and Cash sat on the other.

"What?" he asked.

"I was raised to be a proper wife," she said. "You know, I'm sure you've run across references. Never complain about anything, always welcome him home with a smile and dinner, make sure he has a relaxing evening…"

"Where were you supposed to fit into this picture?"

"That *was* how I was supposed to fit in."

"The perfect doormat."

She winced, not liking the reference, but unable to deny it. "It was all about making him look good, making sure he didn't have to waste any energy dealing with unimportant things."

"You weren't important?"

"I wasn't looking at it that way," she admitted. "He was going to be a senator. That's an important job. I was supposed to do my share to help him get there, and stay there. That seemed important enough."

"I guess it could be. But it's hardly fair to you. You must have had desires and needs of your own. Things you wanted to do with your life."

"I never thought about it. Maybe that's the stupidest thing in the world, but I just never thought about it."

"It's not stupid, but if you ask me it's from another era."

She sighed and folded her hands over her stomach, feeling the infinitesimal pokes from her child. "What would *you* want from a wife?" she argued. "A helpmeet. Someone who could take some of the work around here off your shoulders. What's so different?"

"I would hope that a woman who wanted to be my wife wanted to do those things. I lost one because she didn't. I'm not going that way again."

"Well, it's the same thing."

"Maybe. Maybe not. I'd like, eventually, to find a woman who would be as happily involved in making this place work as I am. I know they're out there. I meet them often, already married unfortunately. But it takes a special kind of woman to want to be a rancher's wife. A corancher, if you will. A true partner. It's a hard life."

"It's a busy life, that's for sure. I see how hard you work."

He leaned forward a bit. "Tell me why you wanted to get involved in the bookkeeping. Was that just to keep busy, or did you like it?"

"I liked it, actually. It was fascinating, and I'd like to learn more. I'm enjoying learning to cook and clean from Hattie, too. Not just because I need to learn, but because it gives me such a sense of accomplishment. Next week she promised I could make a dinner all by myself. I'm really looking forward to that. Imagine a night without a warmed-up casserole."

He chuckled. "She's a wiz with those casseroles, but I have to admit, I sometimes get hungry for a meal that isn't in a single dish."

"I'll do it," Hope said firmly. "I will."

"I believe you." He glanced at her hands. "Is the baby moving?"

"Quite a bit. It's still so small it's hard to feel, though."

He hesitated. "Could I feel? I used to love that when Sandy was pregnant."

For some reason, she didn't even hesitate. She reached for his hand and pressed his palm to her abdomen. "Just be patient," she said.

The warmth of his touch sent delightful shivers through her. Just like his hug, earlier this past week when she'd fallen asleep in his embrace. Amazingly, what Scott had done to her didn't seem to have made her afraid of every man's touch.

Somehow, Cash had escaped the class of predator in which she had placed Scott. Because he had a daughter he was so worried about? Or was it something else about him? She closed her eyes, enjoying the moment of intimacy, hoping there could be more of them. All she knew was that Cash didn't feel like a threat. She wanted him to go on touching her, touching her in other ways, as well. She just didn't know how to tell him that.

"Aww," he breathed as he felt the first little movement, not really a prod, not yet. "It's amazing."

Smiling, Hope opened her eyes. "Isn't it?"

"It's wonderful." He smiled back at her, but didn't remove his hand. "Soon I'll be able to let you feel the same thing in my cows. Interested?"

"Absolutely. And if I'm here long enough, I want to see them give birth."

"Well, that's not necessarily for the squeamish. Sometimes we have to help."

"I don't think I'm squeamish."

He laughed, withdrawing his hand. "I guess we'll see. It's going to be an overwhelmingly busy time for about six weeks. We try to bring the heifers into pregnancy early because they tend to have more problems with the first calf, so we try to stagger things. Heifers first, then the experienced breeders. It kind of makes things go on for a long time."

She barely heard him. Her entire being seemed to have focused on the withdrawal of his touch. She wanted it back. She wanted him to touch her. Mostly, she thought, she wanted to be able to share the miracle inside her with someone, a joy that had been denied to her, but it was more than that and she knew it. Her breathing speeded up with longing, and fear that that longing would not be met.

"Hope? Talk to me. You're...nervous."

He'd wanted her to be honest with him. She just wondered if she could. Expressing her own needs had been denied to her for a long time. When she *had* tried to express them about Scott, she'd met with fury, dismissal and house arrest. The whole experience hadn't encouraged her to express anything. Her hands fisted and she closed her eyes, seeking courage. Inside her, her child moved, reminding her that courage had brought her this far. Now she was sitting with a man who made her aware that she had other needs, who caused her heart to race and her body to ache hungrily. She needed to reach for him, for freedom, for a future.

"I…liked it when you touched me. When you hugged me."

She heard him draw a deep breath. "That's dangerous," he murmured. "I told you I'm attracted to you. I can behave myself but only to a point. Are you sure you want to risk it?"

"I need to," she admitted, her voice cracking. "You wanted to know what I really think. I'm telling you. I thought I'd never want a man again, but I've been wanting you since I first set eyes on you. I need to know."

There, it was out in the open. No escaping back into her carefully maintained facade. She'd just expressed the most basic of human needs; she felt emotionally naked and frankly terrified. Terrified that he might turn her away.

Instead, he astonished her by sliding over and wrapping his arms around her. She sagged into him, melting, feeling so wonderfully welcomed. As if she'd found a new and better place, one she never wanted to let go of.

"Ground rules," he murmured. "You draw the lines. What you say goes. I don't want to scare you all over again. Clear?"

She managed a nod against his shoulder.

"I mean it, Hope. You've been hurt once. I don't want to add to it."

She didn't think he could. He wasn't that kind of man. But she'd been wrong about a man before. The thought caused a little trickle of ice in her, but it quickly vanished in Cash's embrace. He wasn't pressing her in any way, simply holding her. There was nothing to fear in that.

But she had to know how broken she was. She had to know what love would be like with Cash. Mostly, she wanted Cash. All this week that desire had been growing in her, quickly swept under her mental rug, the one that allowed her to present that smooth face to the world.

That rug had been slowly shredding for months now, and it seemed to be completely gone. Rightly or wrongly, she had become raw nerve endings. Exposed and needy.

Life had taught Cash that many a man could screw up, and avoiding mistakes had become a major goal with him. Not only for his ranch, but in his personal life. Sandy leaving and taking his daughter with her had nearly gutted him, and he'd had plenty of time to think about where he'd gone wrong. The problem was, he couldn't change his situation or who he was. He was a rancher, he'd always be a rancher. Unless some windfall came his way, his workload would remain heavy. This was no nine-to-five job.

But he could avoid repeating his mistakes, and he wondered if he was about to make a huge one. There was no escaping his desire for Hope. It had awakened in him almost from the instant he'd brought her home, and it remained hot within him. But he knew he didn't have to give in to it. He didn't have to make a mistake.

But Hope was asking him for it. He hadn't encouraged it in any way that he could see, yet she wanted him. Maybe she only wanted to find out how damaged she was. If so, he ought to back out of this right now. He didn't want to turn into a bad lesson for her. He'd hate himself.

But she had said she wanted *him*. He was no saint, and given that they both wanted the same thing…well, being wanted in return by this woman was something he hadn't even allowed himself to wish for. Not really.

He'd considered her too fragile, which maybe wasn't fair to her. She'd proved herself to be anything but fragile, taking off on her own with no plan except to keep her child. He couldn't imagine the kind of courage she'd needed to stand up to the pressure she had faced, and then flee all on her own.

"Do you do know how strong you are?" he murmured.

"Running isn't usually considered strong."

"It is when it's your only out. I can't imagine withstanding months of pressure to marry the guy or have an abortion. If you weren't strong, you'd have gone one way or another."

"I had to save the baby. And I couldn't stand the sight of Scott anymore. This was the only other option."

"It had to be scary."

"It was," she admitted.

Now here she was in his arms and the urge to protect her nearly overwhelmed him. But was he truly protecting her if he gave in to the passion that pounded in his blood? Because he was hotter than a bottle rocket all of a sudden, hungering for her in a way he had seldom hungered for anyone. Everything about her called to him, made him hot and heavy.

But that wasn't enough, was it? Maybe for her it would be. Maybe she just needed to know that she could still find love and security in a man's arms. A simple enough thing, but it must look like a huge mountain to her after Scott. She might just need to test the waters and discover if she had hope for a normal life after all this.

He didn't know if that would be enough for him. He had his own experience of love and loss to act like an alarm. Could he make love to this woman only to wake in the morning and find she was done with him, sure only that she wasn't completely broken?

He'd survive it, he decided. She hadn't been around so long that he couldn't recover when she moved on. But other doubts filled him, too. This woman had been violated in a horrible way. What made him think he could do the right things to help her heal?

His inability to reach his own daughter was enough to make him wonder if he was nuts to even consider riding into this situation like some kind of rescuing knight. He was no knight, just a rancher, and this could be well above his grade.

But she felt so soft and welcoming within his arms. He became acutely aware of the mounds of her breasts, her curved hip, the gentle swell of her pregnancy. She fit against him as if she belonged there.

"Cash?" she whispered.

"Easy. I'm trying not to rush my fences here."

"Is it that hard?"

"Damn it, you'd better believe it. I'm so hot for you I could start a forest fire on a wet day."

Amazingly, he heard her giggle quietly. "That's a nice thing to say."

"It's true." It was. The drumbeat in his blood was

growing stronger by the second, and he was trying to cling to the shreds of sense. They seemed to want to dry up and blow away before the fire in his veins. The throbbing between his legs was driving him harder than a racehorse in one direction.

Slow. He had to take this slow so as not to inadvertently bring up memories of her bad experience. God, this was going to be hard.

He felt her hand move, then froze with astonishment. As bold as you please, she slid her hand between his legs and cupped him.

"Oh…" she whispered.

He squeezed his eyes shut and tried not to stiffen. "You're playing with fire."

"I never have before," she murmured. "I like it. You want me."

"Didn't I say so?" He pried his eyes open to look into her face. Her eyes were closed, but she was smiling, damn her. "Hope, what the hell?"

Her smile faded a little.

"Talk to me," he demanded hoarsely.

"It's hard to talk."

No kidding, he thought, as her hand squeezed him gently. At that moment she could have led him around by a nose ring.

"I was…I was a virgin. I never ever…" Her eyes opened sleepily. "I never even fooled around in the backseat of a car. I want to know…I want it to be like it is for everyone else."

"I don't want to scare you."

"Scott scared me. You're different."

It sounded so simple. He was different. Of that he was sure, but he was so acutely aware of the hurdles they might face here…

"Cash, take me. Show me."

Well, no man could resist that unless he'd been gelded. A willing woman, passion thrumming hotly through him, no secrets left given where she was holding him...

Hoping he wasn't making the biggest mistake of his life, he pulled away from her, then scooped her up off the couch and carried her upstairs. He'd wanted to know what she was really thinking behind that always-smooth facade, and he'd just found out.

She wanted to be loved like a woman. Like any woman, by her choice. Soon enough he'd find out if Scott had left a minefield behind.

Hope felt an amazing thrill as Cash lifted her easily and carried her upstairs. She wondered if she was losing her mind, but one thing was certain: she wanted Cash. And now that she was no longer hiding from it, she knew the strength of her desire for him.

She wanted him. She had never wanted Scott this way. She'd seldom felt anything for him approaching the hunger that Cash awoke in her. And to think she had been planning to marry Scott. The thought appalled her.

Later, she told herself. Think about what that meant later, think about the way she had been funneled into an engagement that had been nearly passionless. She'd been serving a purpose, but that purpose had had nothing to do with what she needed or wanted.

Maybe she *had* pushed Scott to the brink with her coolness. Not that that excused rape, but she certainly had never felt for him what she was feeling now. He must have known it.

But later. She could think later. Right now she just wanted to be alive, to experience, to discover.

Cash lowered her carefully to her feet, then gripped her shoulders. "Hope? If you're going to change your mind, now would be the time."

She wasn't going to change her mind. Nothing could stop the tsunami that was sweeping through her.

She'd seen his bedroom before, with its big bed and dark colors. If his wife had left any signs behind, they were long gone. This was a man's room.

But she hardly noticed it. She looked up into his weathered face and brilliant blue eyes and felt certainty nail her feet to the floor. Raising her arms, she laid her hands on his shoulders. "My mind is made up."

And the rest of her was trembling from nerves, hope, need, anticipation. She wondered how long her legs would hold her.

He bent his head slowly, as if to give her time to flee, then his mouth settled gently over hers. From that very instant, Hope knew this would be a totally new experience.

Men, she had always thought, seemed to think that a kiss needed to be hard to show passion. Invariably her lips would get crushed, and her mouth plundered, and she didn't especially enjoy it. Not her first kiss, so long ago in college, and not her last. In fact, her experiences had probably been the leading reason she had remained a virgin until Scott forced himself on her. If the rest of the experience was like that, who wanted it? Scott had made the rest of the experience very much like that.

She couldn't imagine why she was allowing her attraction to Cash to push her forward into something she had never before enjoyed. Was she hoping to find out that she'd been right all along, or that she'd been wrong? She honestly didn't know. She had all the normal urges—she just didn't want them answered. Until now. Now compulsion seemed to be driving her.

But Cash approached her differently. His mouth nestled against hers, as if her lips were a delicate flower full of nectar he wanted to sip. It was such a supple, warm feeling that she reacted in a way she never had before. She felt herself grow soft and still inside, as if she were chocolate melting in the sun. Even as she softened and began to feel all warm and gooey, the twinges she had felt between her legs began to transform into a slow, steady throb. Soon, she was sure, her legs wouldn't be able to support the weight that seemed to be growing between them.

He didn't devour her, not in any way. He held her shoulders, steadying her, but didn't swallow her in his arms. He kept sipping at her lips, ever so carefully sucking them and licking them with the tip of his tongue until they became exquisitely sensitive, a part of the passion that steadily overtook her.

At last she could no longer contain herself. She slipped her arms around his neck and responded in kind, giving him the same light kisses. As she did so, she brought the entire length of her body into contact with him.

Hard met soft and a fuse ignited. All of him was hard, like a rock wall, but it felt so good to be pressed against him. All those muscles...for the first time a man's strength seemed to promise safety.

A sigh escaped her, and her mouth opened, inviting him. He took the invitation carefully, sliding his tongue slowly past her teeth, tangling with hers. This was a *kiss*? Her mind spun even as the ache inside her built.

He lifted his head, and she forced her eyes open, a

shaft of fear piercing her. She didn't want him to stop. Not now. A whole new world was opening to her.

But he cupped her cheek in one of his work-roughened hands, brushing his thumb over her cheekbone, smiling sleepily. "Okay?" he asked hoarsely.

"Better than okay," she answered honestly. She pulled her arms down from his neck and gripped his narrow hips as if she would pull him inside of her. Between them a baby stirred.

Feeling it, he lowered his hand and pressed it to her belly, smiling a little more broadly. "I'll be careful."

She was now as sure of that as she had ever been of anything. Impatience began to grow in her. She wanted, needed, *had* to have answers to the ache that pounded inside her, the desire that had blossomed like a full red rose, the answer to promises that had been made but had never before in her life been kept.

Whoever she had been before, she now became a woman in the most basic way possible, needing to have a man buried deep inside her, sweeping her away to mysteries she could only imagine. Everything else vanished before the forces unleashed in her.

"Steady," Cash murmured. "I'm going to unwrap you like a present."

At first she knew a moment's confusion, but then he reached for the snaps on the front of her shirt. She felt the slightest qualm as she realized she would be naked with this man. Hell, she hadn't even been fully naked when Scott forced himself on her, and now her figure had changed and…

"Hope?"

The question reached her. She realized she had looked down and closed her eyes.

"Are you sure?"

She slowly lifted her gaze, battling back the aching web of need and fear that seemed to be engulfing her. "Cash?"

"Yes, sweetie?"

"Can we just... I need to move fast. Things keep... I don't want to get scared or change my mind. I want you."

His face softened. "The whole point of going slow is to let you change your mind."

"I know. I... Just please, show me now, show me fast. Slow can come later."

Cash, who felt like one great big nerve ending of passion, hesitated. He wanted to dive into her like a swimmer coming off the high board. But he understood her fears; he'd been trying to ease her into this. Now she wanted him to just love her right away so that she *wouldn't* change her mind?

She had a hump she needed to get over, he realized. A major one. Maybe she felt it would be easier to just jump and see what was on the other side.

He knew it would be a risk. One wrong move on his part might cast her back into a nightmare. He didn't want to accidentally do that to her, to make her even more messed up.

This time, the lady was asking, and she must be asking for a reason.

"Okay," he said finally. "But you tell me if I do one thing that disturbs you, no matter how tiny."

He felt a shiver course through her, and a sigh escaped her. "Just love me as if you loved me."

Given that her one experience had been rape, he supposed that wasn't the highest bar in the world. He gently maneuvered her over to his bed and urged her to sit.

Then he stepped back and began to shed his own clothes. If she was going to panic, this would do it, he reasoned. To be honest with himself, he knew he was rapidly reaching the point of no return. If there was going to be panic, he wanted it now.

His shirt went flying to a corner of the room. His undershirt followed it. He heard her draw a sharp breath, but ignored it. He reached for the snap of his jeans, paused just a moment, then took the plunge. Less than a minute later he stood before her fully naked, his raging erection plain for her to see.

Only then did he look at her.

She stared at him. He couldn't quite read her expression, but her mouth hung open a bit, and her eyes ran over him, every bit of him. He felt the touch of her gaze as if she was painting him with fire.

"You're beautiful," she whispered finally. "Perfect. I'm not..."

"Oh, hush," he said. He hoped he didn't sound brusque, hoped a little humor tinged the words. At least she didn't quail.

She reached out and nearly threw him over the cliff edge by closing her hand around his erection. He gritted his teeth as warm, soft skin enclosed him.

"You're big," she murmured. "Bigger than..."

Being only human, he couldn't suppress a sense of pride. At least he had one edge over a rich senator wannabe. But there was an important matter at hand. Her hand. "You're driving me crazy."

She surprised him. "Good."

That did it. He tugged her shirt off her, then pushed her back on the bed to yank off her jeans, undies and shoes.

Full breasts spilled free, then her gently rounded

belly, her welcoming hips, her gorgeous legs and most of all her moist center that called to him like a siren.

"You're exquisite," he said thickly.

Her legs still hung over the edge of the bed and he dropped to his knees between them, opening her wide to his view and his touch. Then, carefully, he leaned over her, propping himself on his elbows, waiting for her to meet his gaze. At last she did.

He cupped her face between his hands, then bowed his head down until he nuzzled her breasts. He heard her inhale sharply, then her hands gripped his head, tugging him closer. He needed no clearer message.

Tongue and lips found her nipple, licking and sucking gently. She bucked up against him with her hips. Shifting his weight, he reached down and felt her dewy center. His touch caused a shiver to run through her, one that enhanced his own passion and made him feel good about loving her all at the same time.

"Cash, please…"

The words were suddenly the most beautiful in the world. She didn't want to wait. She really didn't. He hoped he could bring her along with him because every hammering cell in his body warned him that he wasn't going to last long.

Guiding himself, he slid slowly into her. She was tight, so he took care to ease his way. Then, keeping his hand between them so he could gently rub the knot of nerves that would help her through her journey to satisfaction, he began to pump slowly.

Sigh after sigh escaped her, then a cry of astonishment. He gritted his teeth, fighting his own need to erupt, nearly mindless with the pleasure she evoked in him. Her whimpers and moans reassured him, but he had to withhold until…

He felt the orgasm roll through her, felt her entire body convulse with it. Then, and only then, did he plunge one last time and explode, feeling as if his entire being jetted into her.

Pain and pleasure both gripped Hope in those last seconds. She dug her nails into his shoulders, wanting, needing, and not even sure what it was she was pursuing until it hit her, launching her into a place she had never visited before, shattering her in a thousand flaming pieces, and sensation so powerful nothing else existed.

Everything seemed to go black, her body shuddering with completion. Then slowly, ever so slowly, she found herself again, lying beneath the weight of a man who had just showed her that heaven could be here and now.

Little shudders, aftershocks, shook her from time to time, gradually easing. Eventually she became aware that her skin was slick and so was his, that the air felt chilly. That she never wanted to move again.

But he moved her. All too quickly he pulled back, then lifted her. The next thing she was under the blankets with him. He wrapped his arms around her gently, holding her close.

"You okay?" he asked, his voice barely more than a whisper.

"That was incredible," she breathed. "I never dreamed…"

"Do I pound my chest now?"

Much to her amazement, he shifted the mood and she giggled. Actually giggled. "Pound away," she joked.

But there was no chest pounding. Only then did she become aware how tense he must have been, because she felt him completely relax. For the first time she considered that this must have been scary for him, too, making love to a woman whose only experience had been rape.

"Thank you," she said timidly. "Thank you for that. It was wonderful."

"For me, too. Amazing. I was so worried about you, though."

"I could tell. You finally relaxed." She tipped her head a bit to look at him. "Do you think you'll stay relaxed now? Can we do it again?"

He laughed and rolled her over a little, laying his hand on her belly. The baby stirred and his smile deepened. "We can do it again. As many times as you want. We barely scraped the surface."

She burrowed her cheek into his shoulder. "I wondered. I'm sorry I pressed you, but I was so afraid I might get too scared."

"I figured you were trying to get over the hump. I guess you did."

"Completely. After Scott I thought I'd never want to lie with a man like this."

She felt him tense a little again. "How mean was he to you?"

"He hit me," she admitted. "He claimed I was cold, inadequate and that I owed him sex because we were engaged. He never... I mean, he just threw me down, pulled my skirt up and...did it. Then it was over. He stood up, told me to stop sniveling, that I'd better get used to it. Then he just walked out."

"Good God!"

She squeezed her eyes shut. "I didn't want to get used to that."

"Of course you didn't."

"But he was nothing like you, Cash. You were so careful of me, so kind, so…exciting."

"Be careful or you're going to have me wanting to pound my chest again." He gave her a squeeze. "This is supposed to be a beautiful thing, sweetie. It's supposed to bring joy and pleasure to both people. What Scott did was inexcusable. I may have to forgive him, though."

"What? Why?" Everything inside her tightened. Surely he couldn't be excusing that man.

"Because except for his criminality I'd never have met you."

Astonishment filled her, followed by a warmth that penetrated to her very core. "You're a sweet man, Cash."

"Don't put that into general circulation. I'm a tough rancher."

"I'm sure you're both."

He kissed her, another of those light butterfly kisses that ignited her deep inside. Just a few months ago she had been unable to imagine ever feeling this way, ever wanting to be close to a man in this way or any other. Two weeks ago, she had felt as if she were fighting for her very life and the life of her baby.

Now here she was feeling safe and sheltered in a way she had never dreamed possible. But maybe she had never dreamed of feeling this way because she had always been safe, always sheltered and had never imagined needing any more. But she had. Life had taught her that lesson brutally.

It had been a painful awakening, but Cash was right about one thing: she was grateful to have ended up here.

At least for now.

Chapter Eight

Hope would have been delighted to make love again with Cash right away, but she didn't want to press him. A whole, new and wonderful world had opened to her, and she wanted to explore its dimensions while she had the chance.

He seemed to prefer lazing at the moment, and when he at last pulled away from her it was to say, "Let's get a bit of a snack. My stomach's rumbling."

A snack? Really? But then she realized she was hungry, as well. So she didn't object when he went to her room to find her nightclothes and slippers. Once he returned, he dressed her, making it into a devilish delight, brushing his hand, fingertips and lips here and there until she felt as if her whole body was humming. Almost breathless, she said, "If you want to eat, you'd better stop that."

He grinned. "Just making promises for a little later."

Promises? She loved the sound of that. Downstairs in the kitchen, he made her sit then asked if anything didn't sound good to her. "Because," he said, "I want to be bad."

"Bad how?" He was making her smile again. He made it so easy to smile sometimes.

"I want to go into the freezer and get a coffee cake to thaw. Lots of fat, sugar and cinnamon."

"Ooh, that *is* bad," she agreed. All her life she had avoided such foods because they weren't healthful, they might make her gain weight, or—horrors—make her break out. "Yummy. I'm all in."

So he pulled a wrapped coffee cake out of the freezer and put it in the microwave. "Now what do you want to drink?" he asked. "I know you like tea. If I give you milk you might get sleepy."

"I don't want to get sleepy."

He waggled his eyebrows at her. "Good. Neither do I. I wonder if either of us will get enough sleep to deal with all those girls tomorrow."

"Beyond the makeup, I doubt they'll want us around to deal with much."

"True." He laughed and began to brew water for her tea. "Me, I'm having coffee, so look out."

He amazed her with how comfortable he seemed to be with them having become lovers. She'd expected awkwardness, maybe some embarrassment, but there was none. None at all. And certainly he wasn't walking away as Scott had, treating her like trash to be discarded.

The memory darkened her mood. It didn't take Cash long to pick up on it. "Hope? Memories?"

She gave a jerky nod. "Not because of you. Well, maybe because of you because you're so different."

"I'll take that as a compliment." While the micro-wave hummed, the water heated and the coffee brewed, he pulled a chair over so he could sit beside her and put his arm around her. "Want to talk?"

"Why should *he* blight this night?"

"But he already is."

She glanced at Cash, then looked down. "He made me feel like trash. Like something to be kicked to the curb."

His arm tightened around her shoulders. "Can I say I'd like to punch him?"

"Be my guest. I wish I had. I was just so stunned. I don't know how to explain it, but it seemed to happen in slow motion, and yet be over so fast. How is that possible?"

"I guess shocking things can do that to us." He rubbed her arm gently. "I wish I could make it go away."

"I think you have. Most of it, anyway." Then she lifted her chin. "But I wouldn't wish this baby away for anything."

He gathered her to him, until she was sitting on his lap surrounded by his arms. "I'm sure you wouldn't. You didn't fight this hard to keep it just to wish it away."

"No, I didn't." A moment of despair washed through her. "It's going to be hard. I know that, but I'm not sure I can even imagine *how* hard. I have to find work, I have to find someone to watch my baby while I work, I have to…"

"Shh," he said. "First of all, you have a job right here. It's not going away. Secondly, there's lots of help around here and you won't need to leave your baby with some-one else. As for the rest…you've got plenty of time to work it out, Hope. Plenty."

"You gave that to me."

"I'm not sure who gave who what," he replied, a tremor of laughter in his voice.

"But I wasn't trying to get you to say that I'd always have a job here. I wasn't…"

"Shh," he said again, laying his finger over her lips. "I know you weren't asking. You were worrying. Even I can tell the difference. But who knows? You might find out you can't stand it here indefinitely."

Her heart squeezed, because she knew those weren't just random thoughts. He'd had a wife who couldn't stand it here. For him that was a reality, one he couldn't overlook.

He slid her back onto her seat, leaving her feeling oddly bereft, and went to get them coffee cake. Idly she wondered just what a woman would have to do to prove to him that she wouldn't abandon him, then told herself to stop having such ridiculous thoughts. He'd brought her here to look after his daughter, and making love with her—at her request—didn't change the basic facts.

She was probably the last person in the world he would expect to choose life on a ranch permanently. He must look at her and see a mostly useless woman who was accustomed to the finer things he'd never be able to provide. Why would he ever trust her to stay?

Especially if she kept bringing up reasons for him to fire her. She sighed quietly, savoring a mouthful of sinful, sugary delight, and figured she'd better sort out her head while she had time.

She'd been warned in her early education that women tended to attach their hearts to men they had sex with, and men had no such feelings. She needed to guard her heart here and remember that his wasn't at all involved.

Enjoy tonight, she ordered herself. Enjoy this unexpected offering and healing. Tomorrow she'd be back to Angie's problems and her own—deciding the best future for herself and her child. Cash was right about one thing, he was apparently willing to give her all the time she needed—even if she did keep telling him why he should get rid of her.

He was also right about the plastic doll. It was so deeply engrained in her that she was astonished that tonight she had managed to ask for what she wanted. It felt so surprisingly good that she vowed to keep it up.

Maybe little by little she'd find the woman buried under the restricted upbringing.

She lifted her head suddenly.

"What?" Cash asked. He had finished his coffee cake and was now sipping his coffee.

"I was just thinking about trying to find out who I really am after so many years of trying to be what everyone demanded of me. Then I realized something."

He turned to look at her fully. "What?"

"That I found myself over the last four months." A smile began to dawn on her face. "I stood up to them all. I wouldn't let them force me into something I hated. That was *me*."

"It certainly was." He smiled now, too. "Just hang on to that woman. Don't fall back into bad habits. More cake?"

She shook her head. "No, thanks. I'm full now."

"I'm going to have just one more piece, then take you upstairs again for a longer exploration of all your charms."

The words melted her. She was ready to go right then.

This time he led her up the stairs, holding her hand. With each step, excitement grew in her. Her insides fluttered with anticipated pleasure, and she could hardly wait to find out if it would be as good the second time. Or if it would be better.

It was certainly slower. He shed his jeans and T-shirt quickly, as if he wanted them out of the way, but when he approached her, he moved slowly, baring an inch of her flesh at a time, kissing each newly revealed bit. A tug that brought her robe and nightgown off her shoulder, followed by light kisses and a teasing lap of his tongue.

Each kiss felt like a mini explosion between her legs as her body leaped into readiness eagerly. Her robe slipped away until she stood in her thin nightgown. He surprised her then by kissing her and caressing her through the fabric, leaving occasional damp spots behind. The chilliness of them merely added to the heat between her legs, to the exquisite sensations that began to pour through her like hot honey.

He kissed her lips again, lightly as before, until her head sagged back and her mouth opened helplessly. It was an invitation he ignored, instead stepping back a bit so he could fondle her breasts with his hands. The brush of his thumbs over her engorged nipples drew a groan from her and showed her for the first time that her breasts were linked to her very center. Each brush of his thumbs caused a clenching between her legs.

Everything except Cash disappeared from her awareness. She gripped his shoulders to steady herself and let him have his way with her. Her body held secrets he seemed to know but she was only beginning to discover.

Soon her breasts began to ache, begging for more than the light caress of his thumbs. As if he knew it, he bowed his head and pulled one of her nipples into his mouth along with her nightgown. He sucked on her, gently at first, then more strongly until she felt her hips respond, rocking forward with each movement of his mouth. Her entire body seemed to be in thrall to his mouth.

His hands gripped her hips, steadying her. "Now me," he said hoarsely.

With difficulty, she opened her eyes, awash in a tide of hunger. "What..."

Gently he guided her head to one of his own small, pebbled nipples.

She understood at once and swept her tongue over it. The shudder that ran through him emboldened her, and she licked, then sucked. A groan escaped him, and his hand tightened on her head.

Oh, she liked being able to do this to him. Eagerly, she moved to his other nipple, drawing the same response again, feeling for the first time the power of being a woman.

Without warning, he pulled her nightgown over her head, leaving her as naked as he was. Before she could react, he dropped to his knees in front of her.

"Hang on," he muttered to her.

She wasn't sure what he meant until she felt him nudge her legs apart and then bury his face in her dewy nest.

His tongue touched the sensitive knot of nerves and she cried out. Never had she imagined that something could hurt and feel so good all at once. She grabbed his shoulders for fear she would fall over, but he was remorseless.

His tongue was like a lash, lifting her into the farthest reaches of airless space. She couldn't catch her breath. When she found some it was only to cry out as pain and pleasure melded finally into a sensation so exquisite she could never have imagined it.

His name passed her lips like a chant or a prayer. Her legs began to shake before the power of the building sensations deep within her. She didn't think she could survive this.

At last he showed her some mercy, but only to ease her back onto the bed with her hips near the edge, then he resumed licking her in the wickedest torture she had ever known. Her mind seemed ready to explode from an overload, then it quit completely, leaving her mindless with the need he drew out of her.

At that moment she wouldn't have known if the house collapsed on her. She just never wanted it to stop.

Finally, finally, when she was sure she couldn't bear another moment, she crested, feeling like a rocket that shot over the moon only to find herself falling... falling...oh so gently falling back to earth.

Cash gathered her to him under the blankets feeling pretty pleased with himself. He knew where he had taken her. She hadn't concealed that from him at all. Enslaved by the passion, she had shared it with him in her quivers, her cries and her paroxysms. He was quite certain no one had ever showed her *that* before.

Sandy had been a fair lover, but kind of a selfish one. The other occasional ladies over the years had been more skilled at pleasing him, but had given him little of themselves.

This untutored young woman had just given him the greatest gift of all: her unadulterated, unconcealed response. She had journeyed without restraint, and damn, that was wonderful.

He wondered if she would fall asleep. She certainly felt limp in his arms. It was okay if she did because at the moment he was feeling almost like a superhero.

Eventually she stirred a little and murmured something.

"Hmm?" he said. "I didn't hear you."

"What about you?" she said. Her voice still quivered and she still sounded a bit weak.

"I'm fine. Better than fine, actually. But if you want, have your way with me."

She didn't respond immediately and for a few seconds he wondered if he had frightened her.

"I don't know how," she said in a small voice.

"Oh, that's easy," he answered. "When you get your energy back, just explore me. Learn me. Find your own way around."

At that her head lifted, and for the first time their gazes met. "Find my own way around?" she repeated, sounding as if her energy was returning.

"Sure. I'm already hot. Anything you do is only going to make me hotter."

A slow smile dawned on her face. "Really?" It almost sounded like a purr.

"Yeah, really. Or not. Up to you."

"I thought we were in this together."

He chuckled quietly. "*We* definitely just made love. You don't think you were alone, do you? Funny, but none of that would have happened except for the two of us…"

She interrupted him, giving his shoulder a gentle shove. "That isn't what I meant, and you know it."

He just winked at her.

She rose up on her elbow. "You're feeling pretty good right now."

"No kidding. Nothing quite like reducing a woman to a quivering mass of happiness to make a guy feel like a million dollars."

She blushed faintly. "I want to give you what you gave me."

"Have at it," he said, and threw the blankets back. "I'm all yours."

She bit her lip, studying him, and he wondered if she would lose her nerve. He hadn't been kidding when he said he was already hot. His erection throbbed demandingly, and he could easily have just rolled over and taken her. But he wanted to see what she would do.

Hanging on to his urges wasn't easy, but he felt she needed the freedom to take what she wanted on her own. To decide for herself where they would go next. To discover her own powers. It wouldn't take much.

All of a sudden she looked impish. "Well, I know you like this." She brushed her fingers over his nipples. He stirred with pleasure. "And this." She closed her hand around his erection, and this time a moan escaped him.

But then she pulled her hand back. "But what else?" She seemed to be pondering, and he had to force himself to hold still. Wait. Just wait.

In one smooth movement, she rose up and straddled him. The sight of her above him was almost enough to push him over the edge. Her breasts, perfect in every respect, hung over him. Looking down he could see her spread legs and the thatch of hair it would be so easy to reach out and touch.

He had a moment when he wondered why he was being stubborn about this. When he just wanted to let go and take her. But then she lowered her head and kissed him, and as she did so her breasts grazed his chest. The touch seared him like flame. Then her kisses moved from his mouth, down his shoulders, sprinkling more sparklers over his skin. He could feel his manhood leap in response to every touch.

She toyed with his nipples until he groaned help-lessly again and again. Then she rescinded that delight and began to move her mouth lower, across his abdomen. He bucked gently a few times, but anticipation was beginning to overwhelm him. He knew exactly where she was heading. He just wondered if she would have the nerve to do it.

Wondering held him suspended between heaven and hell. He gritted his teeth, fisted his hands and clung to his self-control like a tightrope walker without a net.

His blood pounded in his ears, his loins ached maddeningly, overpoweringly. Twizzles of electricity wormed through him. He'd never really surrendered himself this way before, and he wasn't sure he'd make it. He could just erupt right now before he found out...

Then she did it. He felt it instantly like an electric goad. Her tongue touched his member, then her lips followed. He waited in unbearable uncertainty, afraid Hope might pull away.

But she didn't. Moments later, she claimed as much of him as she could, taking him deep within her mouth. It was hard not to press deeper, when all he wanted to do was plunge all the way, but he held himself still even as moans of pleasure let her know how much he was loving this.

She pulled back, then took him inside her again. Several more times and he was lost. His release seemed to go on forever, but as completion finally filled him, bringing him back from flight to the ground, he realized she was still there, still loving him...

He groaned again and rolled her over, kissing her deeply, the taste of her still rich in his mouth and now mingling with the taste of him in hers. Their tongues tangled, her arms welcomed him, until at long last he sagged, simply content to hold her close.

He wanted this night to never end. But it would, just like everything else.

He brushed away the gloomy thought and gave himself over to the miracle resting in his arms.

Everything changed in the morning. It had to. Cash still had chores, and while he lingered with her over breakfast and apologized a million times and kissed her a million more, cattle couldn't wait.

Hope knew a selfish moment of disappointment, but she understood. She really did. She might emotionally feel as if she ought to be on a honeymoon, but she wasn't. Neither of them were. Work needed doing, and she had to get ready for the night's invasion.

Hattie had done the shopping as usual, laying in a large quantity of snacks and soft drinks, and some frozen pizza. She'd also picked up some cute paper plates and napkins to make it all feel more special.

Hope chose to use the dining room. It had not been used once since her arrival, and she could understand why. The table would seat twelve, and despite the evident age level of everything in the room, it was a very formal place. Not a good choice for three people who were eating a warmed-up casserole.

But it would provide enough room for the makeup demonstration. She just wished she had more than one lighted mirror, but supposed they would manage by taking turns.

As she busied herself, however, her thoughts kept lingering over the night just past. Sometimes things so special happened that she wanted to relive them again and again, as if by doing so she could embed them permanently in memory in every shining detail. Like the time she had won the dressage competition. How many times had she relived that moment?

This was even more special. Her mind lingered over every remembered touch, every remembered sensation. Cash had opened a whole new world to her, and she suspected there was even more.

But one thing he had done for certain was to banish Scott's attack. Or at least to diminish it. She felt like a survivor, and what's more, she now believed that life could get better. That she could enjoy it again. That someday a real Prince Charming would sweep her off her feet for real.

Although, at the moment, she was feeling pretty much as if she had been swept away. Nothing would ever look the same to her again. She had found the gold at the end of the rainbow, and it wasn't money.

She laughed at herself, to herself, almost giddy with her sense of self-discovery. She had fled her home with nothing, had fled her abuser successfully, and she had landed safely. When she had set out, there had been nothing but fear and determination to carry her forward into the scary unknown.

Now she had a place, a job and an incredible lover. Even if it didn't last, she had measured herself and found she wasn't wanting.

She wasn't cold, as Scott had claimed. He just hadn't turned her on. The more she thought about it, the less she believed that she had ever loved him. He had just been the right man, more her family's choice than hers, and like some kind of sap she had just followed the road laid out for her, never questioning whether she was doing the right thing. She had been doing the *only* thing.

All of a sudden she felt liberated. Wrapping her arms

around herself, she twirled with the wonderful sense of freedom. She could do it. She could do what *she* wanted. It might not always be easy, but she didn't have to be what anyone else expected of her. Now she could figure out what she wanted to make of her life, build new dreams to explore.

Wow! It was as if the entire world had opened up to her, filled with possibilities she had never before imagined. So many possibilities that she could barely see them. New possibilities of every kind.

She pressed her hands to her stomach and thought of the baby growing within her. This child would never be limited as she had been. She would encourage her baby to try things, to find his or her own way, to meet his or her own needs. She would open vistas for it, not close them down.

The feeling was heady and carried her through the entire morning until Cash came in for lunch. Usually he carried a sandwich or two out with him, but today he had promised to return and he did.

She even gathered her courage and managed to make him a can of soup to go with whatever sandwich he chose. Following the directions was easy, and she wondered why she had ever been intimidated. Because her family had depended on professionals to do all this, and thus had made it seem arcane, especially with a cook who didn't like trespassers in her kitchen?

She was smiling when Cash came through the door, bringing a taste of autumn chill with him. He sniffed and smiled. "Did you get adventurous?"

"I made a can of soup for you. I'm feeling pretty proud of myself right now. Although maybe I shouldn't. It wasn't hard and I'm wondering why I never tried before."

"Assumptions," he suggested. "Besides, hasn't Hattie been teaching you?"

"She's been trying. She moves fast, though, and I'm sometimes overwhelmed because I can't keep up. But she did promise I'd cook dinner this week."

"I'm looking forward to it." Ditching his jacket over the back of a chair, he wrapped her in his arms and hugged her tightly. "Woman, I've been missing you all morning."

He couldn't have said anything more calculated to make her melt. "Nobody ever said that to me before," she admitted as she rubbed her cheek against his shoulder.

"No one?" He sounded astonished. "Not your mother? Not your ex-boyfriend?"

"No one," she admitted. Odd how it felt shameful, as if there was something wrong with her. It felt so good to hear it from him, but it made her feel so lacking that no one had ever missed her before.

"You, my darling," he said, "have been moving in the wrong circles."

That elicited a giggle from her, shifting her mood away from the darker one that had been trying to rise in her. "That's funny."

"Why?"

"Because I was raised my whole life to believe I had to move in the right circles. The approved circles. To hear them called wrong…" Another laugh escaped her. A liberating day indeed.

"Some folks are just stupid," he said bluntly, then kissed her.

In an instant she turned into a puddle. Amazing how he could do that to her, make her melt until she seemed boneless.

But then he put her gently aside. "I would like to continue that," he said, holding her shoulders and looking deeply into her eyes. "Unfortunately…"

"Work, I know," she agreed, hoping her disappointment didn't show.

"Well, we have an invasion coming at three, so I want to clear the decks so I can be around. I don't think they'll want me in the way, but I still feel a need to be in the vicinity. Parents will expect it."

"Of course." She swallowed her disappointment and watched as he helped himself to a bowl of tomato soup and quickly slapped some cheese and ham on some bread.

"Aren't you going to eat?" he asked as he sat at the table.

"Maybe in a little bit." She sat across from him, putting her chin in her hand, filling her eyes with the sight of him.

"So what have you been up to?" he asked.

"I set up the dining room for the makeup show. But mostly I've been walking around feeling liberated."

He arched a brow. "That's an interesting choice of word."

"It's what I feel this morning. Like I left a whole lot of restrictions behind and now everything is open to me. I can do what I want, be what I want…" She trailed off then shrugged. "There's a lot I need to figure out."

She thought his face had darkened a bit, but then he smiled. "The whole world is waiting for you."

"As much of it as I may want," she agreed.

"There's no rush," he said finally. "You need to have the baby first."

She got the sense that she had disappointed him in some way, and wondered if she thought he was getting ready to leave. He'd been so clear that she had a job here as long as she wanted, but maybe he thought she was getting ready to pack and go.

Sandy. Of course. But she didn't know what to do about that. She was in no position right now to promise much of anything to anyone. Certainly not that she wouldn't move on when the time came, even if it seemed unimaginable to her at the moment.

Nor would he trust any such promise from her right now. She hadn't been here long enough to know if this was the life she wanted. Nor had he known her long enough to have any idea if he wanted to keep her around indefinitely. This kind of thinking was pointless right now.

"I have plenty of time," she agreed, hoping to relax him. "All the time in the world. Right now I'm just so happy to be here."

That seemed to lighten his mood. He ate his lunch swiftly, paused to kiss her again, then headed out, promising to be back before the girls arrived.

She stood for a long time at the kitchen window, watching him ride out to pastures she couldn't see from here. Wondering if she'd found her place in the world, or just a brief respite from struggles to come.

How could she possibly know?

Mary Lou and Angie were the first of the girls to show up. With bright smiling faces, they came hurrying through the door, calling out "Hi!" before darting upstairs with Mary Lou's overnight bag. Mary Lou's mother waved from her truck and drove off.

"This should be easy enough," Cash remarked. He had just come in and smelled richly of loam and cattle. "If we can stand the racket, that is."

"That's probably most of the fun."

"Well, they should be busy for hours with makeup from what I saw the other night. I promise to stay out of sight so they don't get nervous about it, but I definitely plan to listen. I had fun hearing you and Angie that night."

"It *was* fun," Hope agreed, although she was beginning to feel just a bit daunted. Teaching five bubbling, active girls the way to use makeup didn't seem like an exactly easy thing.

"You worry about that part," Cash said. "I'm pretty handy at doctoring frozen pizzas, so I'll take over dinner."

Hope hadn't even thought about dinner, and she flushed a little. "I'm glad I'm not trying to do this alone."

"Just consider me your catering service."

She felt a spark of anger at the way he tossed that out, reminding her of her previous life, but the anger faded as she read his face and realized he was just joking. He hadn't meant anything critical at all.

"I'm nervous," she admitted.

"You're not the only one. I've never hosted a bunch of thirteen-year-olds before. I guess this is our trial by fire." He paused. "I better run and clean up a bit so I don't smell like a barn. I promise to be quick."

Not quick enough, she thought as she watched him dash away. He couldn't come back to her quickly enough.

The thought shocked her, seeming to come out of nowhere. A dangerous thought, one that might only bring her more trouble and heartbreak. She laid her hand firmly over her tummy and reminded herself there was only one thing that mattered. She needed to keep her focus.

Last night had been a beautiful revelation, and she honestly wanted to repeat it again and again. But to invest more of herself in what was clearly an uncertain situation over the long term could cause her huge problems. Could cause problems for raising this child.

Setting her shoulders, she got ready for the invasion, brushing away the wisps of beautiful desire that seemed to cling to everything that day. Putting aside what had clearly been a dream.

Reality had harsher edges.

The makeup party went well although it exhausted Hope. Her stamina seemed to have declined some with this pregnancy, but she wondered if anyone but the girls involved would have eventually felt smacked by their level of energy, noise and activity.

They were exuberant on their adventure. They'd brought their own makeup, but it was soon scattered all over the table as they switched items and tried to find colors that suited them better. They paid rapt attention to Hope's instructions, then experimented, anyway, yielding hours of laughter. Those with cell phones took photos of their results, which caused more laughter.

Ruefully, Hope figured it only took about three hours for them to settle enough to get really serious about the makeup. The idea that if they put it on correctly they could wear it to school eventually tamed them and they settled down.

Cash wandered through with plates full of pizza slices, and those vanished as if by magic. Soft drinks evaporated. Energy levels rose again for a while after they ate, but then ebbed. At about eight that evening, with their faces scrubbed clean, they were ready for popcorn and a movie.

Hope was ready for bed. In the kitchen she sagged into a chair with a cup of tea. Having helped the girls pick a suitable movie, Cash appeared a short time later and joined her. This time he sat across from her.

She sighed and looked at him. There was an unusual expression on his face, somewhere between shock and a smile. "Did something happen?"

"Only that my daughter gave me a big hug and thanked me."

Hope's heart skipped happily. "That's wonderful!"

His smile widened. "I think so. That's the first time ever."

"It's really going to get better," Hope breathed, almost afraid to say it out loud.

"It will. But like I said, I expect fits and starts here. By tomorrow night she may remember every reason she hates me. But right now she's a queen bee in her element. She has five other girls telling her how lucky she is to have a dad like me and a companion like you. My stock is up."

"Enjoy it while you can."

He laughed. "I intend to. I also suspect those girls aren't going to fall asleep at a decent hour, so I'll take over when you want to head to bed. You need your sleep."

"We've still got morning to deal with," she said.

"No kidding. Frozen toaster pastries and cereal. No cooking. Moms will be picking them up around nine."

"So early?"

"Church." He paused. "I should have asked if you're a churchgoer."

"I was. Lately I haven't been." She shrugged. "I'll get back to it, I'm sure. You?"

"On and off. Usually there's something here that needs doing, and I can't always get the time. I feel like I ought to be taking Angie, but when it's just me, there's always something."

"Maybe I can help with that."

"If you want. It might be a culture shock for her, though. I gather her mother never took her at all." He reached across the table and touched the back of her hand briefly. "You really look pooped."

"I get tired more easily now. I'll be fine after a little rest."

"They sure kept you busy."

She laughed. "I felt overwhelmed by all that energy. But it was good. They were all nice and a lot of fun."

Giggles and laughs reached them from the living room. Apparently the girls were watching a comedy. *A nice sound*, Hope thought as she settled back in her chair. A delightful sound. Not one she was used to at home, although she'd enjoyed plenty of it during the time she stayed in the dorm at college.

For a little while, all was right with the world.

With the girls in the house, though, there could be nothing intimate between the two of them, and that made her feel a bit blue. So many things they couldn't talk about, and certainly they couldn't explore their attraction. All of that was now on hold, maybe indefinitely. Maybe forever.

She closed her eyes, smothering a sigh, reminding herself to be realistic. A lot of life was bound to be more difficult now, if for no other reason than that her circumstances had changed dramatically. In addition to being crazily attracted to a rancher who had a daughter old enough to know the score if the two of them indulged in anything romantic, and she felt an entire avenue had just been blocked.

But that wasn't fair. She wasn't here as a fiancée or even girlfriend for Cash, but as a companion and care-taker for his daughter.

They probably never should have indulged them-selves last night, although there was no way she could regret it. She still felt like a bud that had finally opened into full bloom, and she wouldn't give up her new knowledge of herself for anything.

In one night, Cash had nearly erased Scott's mem-ory, erased her horrid experience with him. For that she would always be grateful, even if she never had another opportunity to lie in Cash's arms.

"Hope?"

She opened her eyes.

"Are you regretting last night?"

"No!" She straightened immediately. "Oh, no, ab-solutely not."

"You seem lost in some pretty heavy thoughts."

She felt abashed. "Honestly? I was just thinking that there's no way we'll have any more time together."

She watched a smile begin on his face and spread. "Really."

"Really."

"I think we can manage to take care of that." He gave her a wink. "She does go to school."

"And you go to work."

"I might be able to rearrange a few things some-times. Besides, I'm moving into a slower time of year. Just hang in there, sweetie. We'll find a way."

She beamed. "I hope so."

"Me, too." His expression spoke volumes. She felt

that wonderful honeyed trickle of desire again and clamped her thighs together. At that moment, the baby stirred. She laughed quietly and pressed her hand to herself. "There *will* be something between us."

"A very nice something." He paused. "Don't you want to have a sonogram and find out whether it's a girl or a boy?"

"I'm curious, of course, but that's expensive."

"Brad does them in his office. Maybe not that expensive. I'll ask."

Hope hastened to shake her head. "You've already done enough for me. You can't afford my medical expenses on top of everything else."

"We'll see," he answered. "In the meantime, it sounds like the girls are ready to change movies. I'll go deal with that, and you head on up to bed. Maybe I can find a moment later to peek in on you."

She *was* awfully tired. "Call me if you need me."

"Oh, I think I can handle a bunch of happy girls until they crash on the floor. Don't worry about it."

She checked on the crew in the living room, and found they'd already spread out their sleeping bags and pillows, and were sprawled every which way as the movie rolled to its conclusion.

Smiling, she went upstairs, hugging Cash's promise inside her heart. Even if he couldn't peek in on her later, he had said they would try to find time to make love again.

There might be no future in this, but it was still helping her build a new picture for her future self.

Priceless, she thought. *Absolutely priceless.*

Chapter Nine

The girls all departed around nine the next morning. Angie had circles under her eyes from lack of sleep, but she looked happy, really happy, for the first time since Hope had met her. Without having to be asked, she helped straighten up the living room and announced that the following weekend they were going to have a sleepover at Mary Lou's.

Hope wondered if Mary Lou's mother had been notified of this, but she was enjoying Angie's improved mood too much to ask. Together they cleaned up paper plates, leftover food and drink cups, and ran the vacuum. In no time at all, everything was set to rights.

"Thanks for your help," Hope told Angie.

"My friends loved the makeup thing. They want to do it again. Can we?"

"Sure. It was fun."

Cash had already gone out to work, leaving the two of them alone in the house.

Hope spoke. "You look like you could use a nap."

"Later," Angie replied. "It's not like I didn't sleep at all last night."

Hope couldn't imagine that she had cadged more than an hour or two, but wasn't going to argue about it. If Angie sat still for ten minutes, she was apt to go out like a light.

"Hey," Angie said suddenly. "Who's that coming?"

Hope joined her at the living room window. A big black SUV was pulling up the driveway toward the house. "How would I know?" she asked. "I've hardly met anyone around here."

Angie giggled. "A surprise visit. Dad doesn't get too many of those."

Before Hope could counsel caution, Angie darted out the front door. Grabbing a sweater, Hope hurried out to join her. They stood together on the porch and watched the vehicle's approach. For some reason, Hope began to feel a strong apprehension.

"Maybe you should go inside. Or go get your dad."

"Soon enough when we find out who it is. Relax, Hope. Dad's always saying how good people are around here."

But what if this person wasn't from around here? Hope wondered.

The car, with dark windows that concealed its passengers, pulled to a halt in front of them. Hope pulled her sweater tightly around herself, as if it would provide protection.

Then her heart sank and her world began to spin. Climbing out of that car were her parents. Both of them. Then, oh, my God, Scott.

"Hope?" Angie's voice seemed to fade away. Everything went black.

* * *

When she came back to herself, she was sitting on a porch chair. A hand pressed her head down between her knees. Angie, she realized.

"Hope?" came her mother's voice.

"Keep them away from me," Hope said hoarsely. "Away."

"Stay back," Angie shouted. "Just stay back."

"Don't you tell me to stay away from my daughter," came Mrs. Conroy's sharp voice.

Angie bent until her mouth was close to Hope's ear. "That young guy? He's the one who hurt you?"

Hope managed a nod. "I'll be fine in a second."

"Sure." Angie straightened, keeping her hand on the back of Hope's neck. "Stay back or I'll go inside and get the shotgun."

Hope heard her dad swear. Heard her mother start a tirade. Heard Scott say nothing at all. And all she could feel was a combination of horror that they were here and astonishment that Angie was talking about getting a shotgun. Had the world gone mad?

Then came the most beautiful sound in the world. Cash's voice from the far side of the house. "What the hell is going on?" he demanded.

"Who the devil is *he*?" demanded Hope's father.

"I might better be asking you. You're on my land."

Slowly, shrugging off Angie's hand, Hope straightened up. Like some icon of the Old West, Cash moved forward astride his horse, clad in jeans and a shearling jacket and cowboy hat. When he halted, he was pretty much between the women on the porch and Hope's pursuers. There was no mistaking the shotgun holstered on his saddle.

Hope felt the briefest flicker of amusement. Her

family might be from Texas, but this was a sight they weren't used to, anyway. They were city people.

Then she forced herself to face her parents. They appeared as if frozen in time. Her mother, perfectly put together as always in a tweed suit and pumps, every one of her blond hairs in place. Her dad, wearing a suit with a Western string tie, still tried to look as if he starred in *Dallas*. She couldn't bring herself to look at Scott, but she didn't need to. He was undoubtedly every bit as perfect with his dark hair and gray eyes. He'd always been perfect...at least on the outside.

But looking at her mom and dad hurt. They had wounded her, showed her how little they cared about her, yet she still loved them. Was that sick?

"Dad," Angie said, "these are Hope's parents and the guy who, um, hurt her."

Hope had the pleasure of seeing shock strike her family and Scott, of hearing sharp intakes of breath.

Her father took a step forward, then halted abruptly as Cash's mount moved toward him, clearly blocking him. "I don't know what kind of lies she's been telling you, but we want to take our daughter home. You have no business stopping us."

Cash shifted in the saddle, looking at once relaxed and threatening. "Last time I heard, grown women make their own decisions. Whether she goes anywhere is up to her."

"So you swallowed her lies!"

Cash tilted his head. "Her lies or lack of them have nothing to do with this. She makes her own decisions. That's the beginning and end of it."

Hope's father looked past him at Hope. "You're ruining me with your misbehavior."

Hope felt her jaw drop. Pain and shock warred in her.

Her heart galloped so fast she wondered if it would explode. "I thought I was saving you any more problems. I'm gone. There's nothing for you to cover up now."

Scott finally spoke. "You're ruining him. Do you have any idea how much money your father borrowed from me?"

Another icy river of shock poured through her. Her dad was borrowing huge sums of money?

"You owe me," Scott said. "You get rid of that baby so you can't threaten my career or I'm going to see that your parents live on bread and milk."

Oh, God. Hope suddenly felt sick enough to vomit. "I hate you," she mumbled.

"I'm not real fond of you, either. I don't want you back. I only wanted you in the first place because I thought you'd be the perfect wife for my career. But that kid will always be a threat to me."

"No! I won't tell anyone."

"You already did. Anyway, as long as it's around, you could ruin me with a paternity test. I'm not going to allow that."

The threat acted on Hope like a tonic. All of a sudden, steel replaced the ice in her veins. She couldn't believe she had ever been deluded enough to think she loved Scott, or that he could make her happy. He was simply an ugly, cruel, self-absorbed man. Anger began to replace shock. She stood up. "You don't own me. I am not giving up this baby. I won't get rid of it to protect your name. You'll just have to trust me."

"Trust you?" He sounded scornful. "You'll be holding a sword over my head for the rest of my life."

"Then live with it," Hope said. "I'm through with you and everyone else dictating to me, and I'm not giving up this baby for anything. You might remember that

I didn't want to have sex with you. Not at all. If you hadn't forced yourself on me, this wouldn't have happened. So just live with it."

She realized she was shaking, and she sat quickly on the chair for fear she might collapse. Standing up to them had become a pattern for her, but this was the hardest time ever. Her parents would be ruined? The guilt began to overwhelm her. Their entire lives revolved around being members of wealthy society. She doubted they could survive losing everything. Maybe she was being selfish beyond belief. But then she remembered her child.

"I'll call their note," Scott said.

"No, you won't." She sounded almost frail, but she reached for her strength, strength that had got her through all of this so far. Her voice steadied and grew firmer. "You won't because if you do, I *will* tell everyone what you did. I *will* demand a paternity test. Here you are, Scott. Here's your chance to buy your way out of this. I swear I'll never come after you if you don't hurt my parents."

"Why should I believe you?"

"Because, unlike you, I have honor."

Scott hesitated. At last he said, "One peep out of you and I'll destroy them. I'll destroy you, too, come to that. I'll drag your reputation through the gutter."

Then without another word he climbed back into the car. After a moment, Hope's mother joined him. That left her father, who glared at her. "Don't come home," he said. "Don't ever come back. I never want to set eyes on you again."

He climbed in, slammed the car door and gunned the motor as he sped away.

Angie, Cash and Hope remained in frozen tableau

until finally Hope's anger and shock gave way to tears. It was over. Then why did it feel so bad?

No one said much for quite a while. They all moved inside. Cash seemed to think he needed to hang around rather than head back out to work, and even Angie appeared reluctant to disappear into her room, her favorite hidey-hole.

Hope curled on the sofa, Cash brought her tea, then they all just sat in silence. What could be said, anyway? Hope felt as if her heart had been shredded once more, but she refused to give in again to tears. They weren't worth it, she told herself stoutly. Her father never wanted to set eyes on her again? After that, the feeling was definitely mutual.

She had thought the worst was over, at least with regard to her family and Scott, but she had been wrong. She couldn't believe they had tried to force her to come back with financial threats.

"Sheesh," Angie said, breaking the silence at last. "Money? What did they do? Auction you off?"

"It feels like it now," Hope admitted. "I'm sorry you had to hear all that. You should have just come inside."

"I'm glad I didn't miss it. I need to know how messed up people can be, and that was messed up. Besides, that Scott guy is like Mom's old boyfriend. It's not like I'm innocent."

That gained Cash's immediate attention. "What the hell happened?"

Angie shrugged. "Oh, some guy tried some moves on me two years ago. Mom got a restraining order against him."

Cash looked poleaxed. "Nobody told me."

"What were you going to do about it? She did everything. I'm fine."

"Fine? Are you sure?" He was half out of his chair. "I'll kill him."

"No need, he's gone." Angie shrugged again. "Really, I'm fine. *My* mother listened to me, unlike Hope's. Can you believe those people?"

Cash shook his head slowly, clearly unwilling to change the subject, but evidently unsure whether to pursue what happened to Angie. "They do strain my credulity."

"That means you can't believe it, right?"

"Right."

"Me, either. Hope, are you okay?"

"I will be." At the moment she didn't exactly feel like it, but she reminded herself she'd been through much worse. Today she had stood up for herself and her baby, and had won. "Thank you both for standing with me."

"Like I was going to do anything else," Angie said. "Or Dad for that matter. We take care of our own, don't we, Dad?"

The most beautiful smile dawned on his face. "Yes, honey, we do. Thank you."

Angie scowled and curled in on herself on the other end of the sofa. "That Scott guy was something else. The only thing he cares about is himself. I *wanted* to shoot him."

Hope drew a breath. "I understand the feeling, but please tell me you wouldn't."

"I wouldn't," Angie said irritably. "Even if he deserves it. But I couldn't believe him standing there demanding you get rid of your baby as if you owed it to him. As if whoever he is is more important. He's an ugly man."

"And you have a fine moral sense," Cash remarked. "I'm proud of you."

A small smile peeked out around Angie's mouth. "I was proud of Hope. She stood there and told him she'd ruin him if he hurt her family. Like her parents deserved her protection." Then she sighed. "I guess I can't tell anyone about this, huh?"

Cash shook his head.

"Too bad. They'd love it. Oh, well." She bounced up out of her seat. "I need a sandwich, then I'm going to do my homework. And no, I'm not going to call all my friends and tell them. I get it."

In the silence after Angie dashed up the stairs with her sandwich, Hope said reluctantly, "You need to get back to work."

"I'm not leaving you alone. My men can handle the little that's left to do today." He moved over to sit right beside her on the couch.

"I'll be fine," she protested, even though she felt as if the whole thing was just beginning to hit her, even though she didn't want Cash to leave her.

"I'm sure you will. Eventually."

He leaned forward, resting his elbows on his knees, and studied her. "I don't even know how to express how appalled I am at what I saw, and I don't even care about those people. You do, or did, and it had to have been a lot harder for you."

"It was a shock," she confessed. "I really didn't think they'd follow me. Or even find me all the way out here."

"I have to admit I'm surprised how quickly they did it. I guess I'll never know how."

"Me, either. I know your sheriff said they could still find me, but..." She shrugged. "I don't get it. The FBI has a harder time finding wanted criminals."

A short laugh escaped him. "True. But maybe you left a trail of bread crumbs."

She thought that over. "Maybe I did, in a way. They canceled my credit cards when I was in Denver, but I still had the debit card from my bank account. I took the last money out of it just the day before you hired me. Near Casper, I think. So they could have gotten pretty close quickly."

"And people around here inevitably talk. A new person would garner some interest."

She nodded. "It was probably easier than I thought."

"Evidently."

She knotted her fingers together. "I'm so sorry, Cash."

"For what?"

"All that ugliness. You and Angie having to see it. The invasion."

The shame. The guilt. All of it was churning inside her, with no outlet, no way to quiet it. Realizing that she had not only been raised like a prize filly, but also evidently auctioned off like one.

"Maybe the money didn't have anything to do with it, Hope." He slipped an arm around her, hugging her.

But looking back, she was almost sure it did. She'd been paraded. She'd been nudged. She'd been practically thrown into Scott's arms by her own parents, who kept telling her it was a perfect match. "I was an idiot," she said. Her breaths speeded up. "I was living a delusion. He was Prince Charming. Everyone had me convinced it was a brilliant match, that I'd be so happy, that…" She trailed off and struggled to maintain control. "I should have noticed the change. Before that, they'd seemed primarily interested that I spend time with the right kind of people, date the right kind of men. They settled on Scott before I did. I was being maneuvered and didn't even realize it. I thought it was that he was going to be a senator. It never occurred to me they might have other reasons."

"Does the reason really matter? If you were guilty of anything it was being conned by everyone you trusted. I think most of us would fall for it."

She lowered her head, almost afraid to look at him, so see his reaction. "I'm that plastic doll you called me. Just put me where you want me and tell me what to do." The bitterness of the words shocked her. But as she looked back at how she had been nudged toward Scott, made to feel as if it would all be perfect for her with him, that she had an important and beautiful future awaiting her as a senator's wife, she couldn't deny that she'd been manipulated, and quite willingly. She had been bred to fulfill the dreams of others.

"What I said..." Cash spoke hesitantly. "I take it back."

Startled, she lifted her head. "What? It's true."

"No, it's not. I found the woman behind the facade the night before last. She's real, passionate, warm and very much her own woman. She had the courage to run from everything she knew to protect her child. And today you were just magnificent. Magnificent."

She shook her head a little. "I thought *you* were magnificent arriving like that on horseback, ready to protect me. Angie was magnificent. That daughter of yours takes after you, Cash. Very much so."

He smiled, tilting his head. "She does seem to, doesn't she? I was proud of her, too."

"I *am* sorry she had to hear that ugliness, though."

"She's taking it in stride, as you noticed. Quite opinionated, too. But what was this about some guy her mother had to get a restraining order against?"

Hope's heart sank yet again. Discomfort made her edge away a little. At once the arm around her loosened, but at least it didn't go away. "She mentioned it to me briefly. I don't know the details. I wanted to tell you, but she was so adamant about me not spying on her." She closed her eyes momentarily. "It made me feel like hell not to say anything. But…what could you do at this point? If I'd told you and you'd said something to her, we'd have lost all trust around here." She peeked at him nervously.

His face darkened briefly, but then he nodded. "I see your point. It's okay. At least she mentioned it herself. I guess she's the one I need to talk to about it."

"Yes, she is." Hope twisted, facing him at last, her courage fueled by his understanding. "She didn't give me any real details. She seems most affected by the fact that her mother stepped in so quickly to protect her. And that all came out when I told her how I'd gotten pregnant."

"She asked?"

"Yes. I kept it as sanitized as I could, but then she told me about what had happened to her. Just the bare outline, and she was gone."

"She can be like that. Dropping a bomb then disappearing." He sighed. "Thirteen-year-olds are fascinating creatures."

He went to get her another cup of tea and suggested she eat something. She answered that she just wasn't hungry, not now, and fresh tea would be great.

But alone in the room, she had more time to think. Time to think about what she'd seen today, a side of her father she had never imagined existed. He never wanted to set eyes on her again? She told herself she felt the same, but the truth was, that had pierced her heart. Through it all, even the ugliness before she fled, she had believed she and her father had had a special connection.

Apparently not. She wondered if she had been harboring some foolish notion that eventually she could return to her family, at least have some kind of relationship with them, once they realized she wasn't going to embarrass Scott out of his political career. Now she knew otherwise.

She had failed them, failed at the one thing they had expected of her. Or maybe, to be honest, she had failed at everything they had expected of her. She wasn't the Triple Crown winner they thought they had raised.

Then a shudder passed through her as she realized how close she had come. If Scott hadn't raped her and made her pregnant, she'd be weeks away from marrying him. Weeks away from starting down a path that she now suspected would have been even harder to escape and probably would have made her very unhappy.

She hadn't been measured for romance; she had been measured for a politician's wife. Scott had only been pretending to love her, and she wondered if she would eventually have become one of those political wives standing by her man as he admitted to one of his indiscretions and claiming he had sorted out his priorities, never to slip again.

Hell, she couldn't even be sure Scott had been faithful to her during their engagement. The doubts had occasionally plagued her, but she had swiftly buried them. She had no evidence, after all.

But she had wondered then, and she wondered now.

She could, she realized, get really hopping mad if she let herself.

But out of the blue, one thing struck her and struck her hard. When she had seen those people, people she had loved, she had felt as if she were looking at aliens from another world. She was no longer part of that, and she never wanted to be again. Strangers. They had become strangers.

Probably because she had never really known them.

"Hope?" Cash stood beside the couch, putting down another cup of tea for her and a small piece of pastry. "You look like you got hit by a train. Again."

"I feel like it," she admitted.

He sat beside her. "What's going on?"

"It just suddenly struck me that my family, Scott... they all come from another world. It was as if I was meeting them for the first time, and I just didn't understand them. I also realized that I never want to go back to that. Ever."

"You don't miss any of it?"

"That's the weird thing. I don't. It's as if I've moved to a whole new world here. I like it. I like being useful and doing useful things. I like helping Hattie, and spending time with Angie and you. I like all the stuff I'm learning around here. I'm sure I'm not much help to you, but I feel more helpful and useful than I ever have. I looked at them and I hardly recognized them."

"That's quite a shift." Nonjudgmental, leaving it to her whether to say any more. Even his expression revealed nothing except a gentleness.

He was, she realized, an incredibly accepting man. "Maybe I've finally figured out what really matters."

"And that is?"

"What you can do for others, however small. Money

doesn't matter, as long as you have the necessities. Beyond that...well, maybe it's all about what you have to give."

He nodded, remaining attentive, awaiting whatever she wanted to say.

"I thought I knew happiness," she remarked. "I didn't. I've found happiness here in such little things. Like teaching Angie about makeup. That was great. The sleepover was great, even if it wore me out. All of it matters more than a balance in a bank account."

A smile slowly creased his face. "I agree. I'll tell you I had some qualms when I first looked into your background. I couldn't figure out how a Texas princess was going to fit in around here. But you have."

"I'm so grateful for the opportunity you gave me. So grateful. I still have a lot to learn, but I never would have imagined I could feel such a sense of accomplishment from making my own bed." She laughed mirthlessly. "Or mopping a floor. I can see the results of what I do, and I like it."

He arched his brow, feigning horror. "You *like* mopping a floor?"

"I didn't say that," she answered, a smile coming to her own face. "But I like what I see when it's done. Such a sense of satisfaction. Do you feel that, too?"

"Around the ranch? You bet."

"Thank you for the tea." She reached for the cup, cradling it in her hands. "I've learned a lot about myself lately. And about others. It's going to take some getting used to."

"Take all the time you need."

Cash had meant it, too, but as the weeks passed he wondered what was happening in his life, in Hope's, in

Angie's. Things seemed to reach some kind of stasis, and he wondered if any of them were moving forward, or just waiting for the next bomb to drop.

Now that she had friends, Angie was a whole lot easier to get along with. She still had her moods, and sometimes blew up at him over what seemed like nothing, at least to him, but she was at long last settling in. She seemed to be fusing a deep relationship with Hope.

He wondered if that was a good thing. Hope would probably be moving on. While she seemed to be settling in at the ranch, and seemed to be mostly happy, he doubted she would want to stay once it became routine for her. Right now it was still fresh. He had only to think of Sandy to know what could happen when it grew stale.

Not that he wanted Hope to go. That worried him, too. Like his daughter, he was beginning to consider her an essential part of his life. Just having her there felt good, and he had no doubt that when she left he'd feel a big hole. He could handle it, but he wondered about Angie. She'd lost enough already.

Then there was his desire for Hope. That wasn't waning at all. Despite his promise to make time for them, he hadn't been able to, probably for the best. He had his own doubts about Hope, but he wasn't the only one he had to worry about. Angie was around most of the time, and he worried what she would think if she knew her dad and friend were having an affair. The rest of the time, work demanded his attention. Unless he married Hope, he guessed he could pretty much forget taking her to bed again. Nor was he ready to consider such a thing yet. He couldn't be sure Hope really wanted this life. How many times, after all, had she suggested she leave? Admittedly, she hadn't done that lately, but that didn't mean anything.

Hope's belly began to swell until there was no hiding her pregnancy at all. Not that he thought it needed to be hidden, but it had certainly engaged Angie's interest. The girl was as full of questions for Hope as a game show host.

Finally, as the days and weeks slid by, he decided he'd been a fool. He'd hired a nanny for his daughter because the girl needed help and companionship, and instead he'd got a whole bunch of other problems. Problems that had never crossed his mind.

Problems like developing emotional attachments that could be shattered the instant Hope decided to move on.

He couldn't believe she would stay. This whole life was different from anything she was used to. Sandy had known what she was getting into and couldn't handle it.

Why the hell would a Texas princess be any better?

At any moment, he half expected her to announce she was going home. Or just going away to someplace less dull.

Living on tenterhooks, wondering if he'd created the potential for another disaster, was killing him. Unfortunately, it was too late. He couldn't protect Angie from loss. Or himself, for that matter.

Sometimes, life just stank.

Chapter Ten

Awareness came slowly, but Hope realized that Cash was withdrawing from her, trying to place a distance between them. After the burst of intimacy, after their lovemaking, things had at first seemed to be growing between them. Increasing closeness. Caring. Maybe it never would have amounted to any more than that, but what she felt now was a distinct chill.

He engaged her in fewer personal conversations. He seemed to be busier than ever, away from the house more than at the beginning. Apparently, he'd lost interest. Maybe that visit from her parents had convinced him that *she* was from another world and would never mesh with his.

She tried to be honest with herself. She was, after all, just his employee, hired to look after his daughter. Their brief fling had been the result of hormones and nothing else. Much as it hurt her to think of it that way, she reminded herself that he'd still given her a great gift, the gift of knowing Scott hadn't ruined her for another man. He'd got her past the worst hump of her rape until these days she could look back on what had happened and understand it hadn't been her fault or her failing. She *was* a good lover.

But apparently not good enough. Or maybe she just wasn't right for Cash.

What was she thinking, anyway? This was a job. She'd needed it, she'd been given it and she should focus on that, not on some crazy illusion she had started to build that she could spend the rest of her life here.

Why had she ever dreamed of that, anyway? Just because Cash had been good to her? Protective of her? Because he took her to the doctor for her checkups?

She tried very hard to remember she was just a hired companion for Angie. She and the girl were getting along fairly well now, and Angie's relationship with her father seemed to have settled a bit.

But as Angie came out of her shell and began spending more and more time with her new friends, Hope was beginning to feel useless in that role. She helped with cooking, she helped with cleaning, she even took over some of the accounting work from Cash, doing it during the days while he was out so he could have more free time in the evenings.

Despite that, he seemed to be finding additional reasons to work late, or disappear into his office.

She couldn't mistake the wall he was building between them as if he had decided it had been a mistake to ever breach it.

She looked down at her swelling belly, as sorrow filled her yet again, and wondered if she should just leave now or should wait until the baby was born. It might be easier for Cash and Angie to settle into a routine before she became a bigger part of it. Yet Angie was so excited about the coming baby she rivaled Hope with her interest.

So she hesitated amid the growing chill. Her bank account could still use some padding, although Cash had been generous enough in paying her. She wouldn't even have expected minimum wage for what she was doing around here, especially since she was getting room and board, but he paid her more than that while taking care of her medical bills.

It was just a job. They never should have crossed the boundary, as he was making clear. The only question now was how much longer she would be needed here. Or even wanted, at least by Cash.

She just needed to tough it out. Mostly for Angie. As for her own feelings for Cash, which seemed to have grown deeper despite everything, she just needed to put them on ice. They could go nowhere. Were going nowhere.

Just a job. She repeated the mantra to herself a hundred times a day and tried to stay too busy to think.

Six weeks after her parents' visit, she answered the phone, expecting it to be Angie saying she wanted to bring a friend over, or spend some of the weekend at Mary Lou's. Those requests were becoming more common, a good sign for Angie.

But instead, she heard her mother's voice. In an instant everything inside her froze somewhere between terror and longing.

"Hope."

For several seconds she couldn't answer. Then, weakly, she said, "Hello, Mother."

"I know…I realize… Well, this has all been terribly ugly."

Something both her parents loathed. Hope braced herself, wondering if she should just hang up.

"We smoothed it over, saying you'd been taken ill and gone to a clinic. Everyone is moving on."

Bitterness turned Hope's mouth sour. "How good for you and Scott." She nearly choked on that man's name.

"Yes. Well. That's not what I'm calling about. It's… Oh, Hope, I don't agree with your father."

Another wave of shock ran through her. She didn't make a sound, merely tried to find a breath so her heart wouldn't stop beating.

"The point is… He might disown you, but I'm not. I can't. I…" Her mother's voice broke then steadied. "I realize you can't come back to Dallas, at least not for a long time but…I want to see my grandchild. I want to see you. So…I'm thinking of flying up there when the baby comes."

Forever passed before Hope could manage to speak. Her heart was galloping like a horse in the Preakness, her breaths came in short gasps, and her entire universe seemed to be whirling. "I, um…I don't know if I'll still be here, but…it wouldn't be my decision. This is Mr. Cashford's home. I would have to clear it with him and…" Something inside her seemed to snap, just a little snap, but it freed her in some way. "I'm not sure myself. I need to think about this."

"Of course you do," Mrs. Conroy said swiftly. "Can I…call again in a few weeks?"

"I guess." It was the best Hope could do. Once again her world was being thrown into a blender and she felt as if everything were topsy-turvy. When she hung up, her thoughts were so scattered she couldn't gather them up.

Her mother wanted to see the child? Wanted to visit? The daughter she had been wanted that so badly. This was her *mother*. But another part of her resisted, reminding her of all the ugliness that had come before her flight. Her mother hadn't defended her then. Not a bit.

She even felt a wave of suspicion. This could be some kind of ploy. Some new angle of attack designed to protect Scott.

God! She put her head in her hands and let the world spin, wondering where or when it would ever settle.

Angie breezed through the door at four, took one look at Hope and dropped everything. "What happened? Is the baby all right?"

"Everything's fine," Hope lied, wondering if her face had turned into some kind of neon sign. Hiding her feelings had long been demanded of her. A smooth, pleasant face at all times. Apparently she'd lost the skill.

"No, it's not," Angie said firmly. She tossed her jacket over a chair, disregarding the house rules she'd been following lately, and grabbed Hope's hand.

"You're coming with me. I know you always want tea, but I have something better."

"What?" Hope asked distractedly.

"Hot chocolate. Chocolate is good for nearly everything that ails you."

A little laugh, more nervous than anything, escaped Hope as she allowed herself to be dragged into the kitchen and plopped at the table.

"My mom taught me how to make the good hot chocolate," Angie said as she began to rummage in the refrigerator. "Lots of cocoa powder, cream, sugar…" In no time at all she was heating the concoction on low heat. "Sorry, it takes a few minutes."

"I'll survive."

"Of course you will," Angie said stoutly. "Besides, we don't have to wait for that to have chocolate." She disappeared into the pantry and came out with a candy bar. Putting it in front of Hope she said, "Open it. I'm going to have some with you."

Hope found herself wondering who was the adult right now. For the first time in a while she felt amusement flicker through her.

"So what happened?" Angie demanded as she stirred the pot on the stove. "Something did."

A lot of things were happening, but Hope seized on the most immediate thing. "My mother called."

"That witch?" Angie turned and looked over her shoulder. "What did she want? Your head on a platter?"

"God, you're too much."

Angie grinned. "And you love it. So?"

Hope hesitated only briefly. "She said she wants to come visit when the baby is born. That she wants to see her grandchild and doesn't want to disown me."

Angie astonished her then. "I bet an invitation to come home wasn't included."

"No. No, it wasn't." This thirteen-year-old was beginning to seem a lot smarter than her years.

Angie shrugged. "Must be fun to be the big family embarrassment. So far I haven't managed that, although I think there were a few times Dad wanted to send me to Antarctica to cool me off."

In spite of everything, Hope felt her spirits lifting. "He'd never do that."

"Oh, I know. I finally figured that out. But I was pretty hard on him, wasn't I?"

"I think he was getting to the edge of desperation."

"Me, too. At the time I liked it. I don't want to make him feel that way anymore."

"You had a lot to be mad about, losing your mother and moving."

"Yeah, I guess. But at some point I realized I wasn't the only one things happened to. You helped me realize that. Bad things happen, right?"

"Sometimes, yes." Inwardly, Hope uncoiled a bit. Apparently her time here hadn't been wasted. She opened the chocolate bar and broke off a piece, then popped it into her mouth. She pushed the wrapper across the table for Angie to help herself.

"Oh, no," Angie said, deserting the stove briefly. She pushed the bar back. "You need more than that to get the benefit."

"You'll make me fat."

"Not a chance. Not even with that baby. Say, when are you going to find out whether it's a boy or a girl?"

"When it's born."

"Got any names in mind?"

That provided a safe topic of conversation until at last Angie filled two mugs with frothy hot chocolate and joined her at the table. "I like it bitter, so if you want more sugar, let me know."

Hope took a cautious sip. "This is great."

Angie beamed. Then she dropped the hammer. "So are you going to let your mother visit?"

"It's not my decision alone," Hope said. "I mean, if I'm still here."

Angie's smile faded and she looked down. "You're thinking about leaving?"

"I'm not sure I'm needed here anymore." It hurt to say it, but it was true. Angie and her father were at last developing a workable relationship, at least when he was around. For Cash's part, he seemed to wish she was already gone. Where did that leave her? Depending on a man's charity until the baby came? Her pride rebelled at that. She was through being "kept" by anyone.

Just then the back door opened. Cash. She heard the familiar weight of his steps, the sound of him jacking his boots off and hanging his jacket. *Time to change subjects*, she thought. She sought for something safe to say, but as Cash entered from the mudroom, Angie leaped to her feet.

"Hope is thinking about leaving!"

Stunned, Hope couldn't bring herself to look up from her mug. Silence filled the kitchen. Apparently Cash hadn't taken another step.

"It's *your* fault," Angie said. "Yours!"

"What did I do?"

"That's exactly it," Angie nearly shouted. "She doesn't feel wanted around here anymore, and it's because of you."

Hope began to tremble inwardly, but she knew this had to stop now. She didn't want to create a rift between Angie and her father. "I didn't say that," she said as clearly and loudly as she could manage.

"You didn't have to say it," Angie went on. "You said you don't feel needed anymore. Well, I know why that is. Dad has been acting like the last place he wants to be anymore is in this house. With you. I'm just a kid and *I* can see it."

Cash didn't answer. Hope felt his silence like lead in her heart. She was about to lose something else, and though she'd been wrestling with her own scattered thoughts, in that instant it all became so clear that she thought the pain of impending loss might kill her.

The baby poked her, hard, but for once she didn't

feel like smiling. She thought she had known pain after the betrayal of her parents and Scott, but this felt a million times worse.

"I want her, Dad. Even if you don't. I like having her here. She makes me feel good. She's a great friend. Don't you dare send her away!"

"I'm not sending anyone away," Cash said in a measured voice. "That's the last thing I'm considering."

"Then maybe you ought to stop acting like we have the plague in this house." With that, Angie ran from the room. Her steps thundered up the stairs, then her bedroom door slammed hard enough to be felt throughout the house.

"What the hell?" Cash said quietly. After a moment, he pulled out a chair and sat. "What did you say to her?"

Hope's hands tightened around her mug. Her stomach roiled until she thought she might vomit. "Very little," she murmured. "That I wasn't sure I'd still be here when my baby comes because I was feeling like I wasn't needed anymore. You guys have a decent relationship now."

"The relationship just blew up. Again." A bald statement without even a hint of sarcasm.

No way could she bring herself to look at him. She had evidently just undone everything they had been working toward, all because she was drowning in self-pity. So the man wasn't paying a whole lot of attention to her. She *was* just an employee, after all. He wasn't required to notice her at all.

"I'm sorry." She hated how small her voice sounded. "I don't know why Angie's blaming you. She really shouldn't. I'm just an employee here and it's not your fault you're so busy."

"It's not busy. She's right about that. I've been avoiding you."

She felt as if a knife stabbed her heart. She squeezed her eyes shut and wondered if she would be able to draw another breath ever again. How had this become so important to her? For weeks now she'd been aware of disappointment that Cash seemed to be so busy, that he might be avoiding her, but hearing it from his lips made it all so real she wanted to scream from the anguish.

When at last he spoke, she could hear how carefully he was choosing his words. That didn't make her feel any better.

"I'm a coward," he said slowly. "I *have* been avoiding you, but not because I didn't want you around. I've been staying away because I want you around too much."

At that, everything inside her went utterly still. She still couldn't open her eyes, though, and she clenched her fists until her nails bit deeply.

"I had one woman walk out on me and take my child with her. I swore that was never going to happen again. Then, like a fool—or so I told myself—I started to care about a woman who had absolutely no reason to want to bury herself on this ranch. You're used to a whole different kind of life, a kind of life I can never offer. But I cared, anyway, and when I realized how much it would hurt if you decided to leave, I decided to…call a halt. To prevent myself from getting any more deeply involved with you. I was afraid. I *am* afraid."

Some of the tightness in her eased, but only a fraction. She thought that was one hell of an honest statement for a man to make. Admitting fear? "Why didn't you talk to me?"

"Because you haven't been here very long. How could you possibly know if you really wanted to stay here? This is so different from everything you've known. Sure, that makes it interesting for a while. Even fun. But then the grind sets in."

"So...you don't trust me?"

"I trust you. I just can't see why in the hell you'd want to bury yourself on this ranch for more than a few months."

A spur of anger kicked her out of her frozen state. She opened her eyes and saw nothing on his face but a kind of sad acceptance. "How about considering that I'm not Sandy? How about asking me how I feel about being here? How about considering that I can no longer imagine any kind of life away from here? I thought about it, Cash, and there's absolutely no place I'd rather be than here. But I don't want to stay if you don't want me."

"Wanting you is not the problem. I want you all right. If it ended there, it would be meaningless, but it goes beyond that. I was building a life that included you, and then I realized you might well not want to be included for the rest of your days. What the hell do I have to offer a woman like you?"

"Like me?" More anger awoke in her. "Like *me*? You apparently don't know me at all. I came here from a different world, but the thing is, I discovered I love this world. I love living here. I love the rhythms of life here. I love the wide-open spaces, the mountains, the animals, your daughter... What do you have to offer me? How about *you*?"

"That wasn't enough last time."

"This isn't last time. This is now. I'm not Sandy— I'm me. I've never felt as good about myself or as happy as I have since I came here. The only thing driving me nuts is the way you're avoiding me. If you'd stop that, I'd have no complaints at all."

"It's too soon…"

"Hogwash," she said hotly. "Just hogwash. The truth is, I never want to leave. I want to raise my child here. If you want to keep on avoiding me, go ahead, but you're not going to get rid of me, not easily. Now that I know what's going on in your mind, I'm not going anywhere. You're stuck with me. Even if you fire me."

When he remained silent, she said, "You were the one who told my parents that a grown woman makes her own decisions. Are you trying to make them for me? Because it feels like it. And what's more, you can't possibly care about me at all if you don't trust my judgment."

Now he looked stunned. She was beginning to feel hopeful, but hardly dared nurse it. He could still tell her he'd just been trying to be kind to her. Could still find a way to worm out of the challenge she had just thrown.

What the hell had come over her, anyway? Standing up for herself regardless of what he believed and wanted? Sheesh, she was throwing herself at the man. She ought to be ashamed. But shame was the last thing on her mind. She was in the fight of her life, a fight every bit as important as saving her child—and her pride could go hang.

Cash rose unexpectedly. Then he took her hand and tugged her. "Come on."

To her surprise he led her through the mudroom and out the back door. Cold air sliced at her instantly, and she knew she'd be shivering in a moment. What in the world?

"Feel that air? Winter's only a breath away. In a few days or weeks, you'll come out here and snow will cover everything. You won't be able to get to town just any old time. You'll have to wait for snowplows to clear the county road and me to clear the driveway. It'll be like that for months, almost completely cut off. I know you get winter in Dallas, but believe me, it doesn't last like winter here. Cabin fever is a very real thing."

"Unless you're with people you care about."

"You'll be alone a lot, anyway. I have a mess of cows to look after. They'll need to be tended, and when they can't graze through the snow anymore, I'll be out there for hours depositing hay and feed. I'll drag through the door at night worn out from the day and the cold, and I'll probably be cussing. All I'll want is a hot meal and a chance to thaw out. You really think you can stand that?"

"Cash…" She wrapped her arms around herself and tried to speak, but already her lips were feeling stiff.

"Come back inside," he said gruffly.

In the kitchen, he didn't hesitate, but took her in his arms, rubbing her gently, trying to warm her. "This is a place for survivors. We make our own amusements when we're not working. It can feel empty and lonesome for long stretches. Hell, ranch wives have been known to go crazy from solitude."

"I was pretty much locked up in my bedroom for four months in a houseful of people who were furious with me. I didn't go nuts."

"Maybe you're strong enough," he admitted. "But is it what you *want*?"

"What I want," she said, lifting her head, "is a chance for a life here. I'm not asking you to marry me. I get that you have reasons to be doubtful, and you probably don't love me, anyway. But I want the *chance*, Cash. The chance to stay here, even if only as hired help, to raise my child here where everything is real and important. To have you as a role model for the baby, a man who's honest, loyal and hardworking. You can give me that chance without committing to anything."

But then it was as if her mind took a step back, and she realized what she was doing. She was pressuring Cash for something he might not want, something that might make him unhappy. What had come over her?

She stepped back far enough that his arms dropped. "I'm sorry," she said. "I have no right to demand anything of you."

"Ah, hell," he said, sounding a bit angry. She saw him run his fingers through his hair. "Ah, hell," he said again. Then without another word he scooped her up in his arms. She gasped and grabbed his shoulders as best she could, hanging on as he carried her upstairs. He set her on his bed, then vanished through the door.

A couple of seconds later, she heard him banging on Angie's door. Then she heard him say, "Don't come looking for me or Hope. We have some things to sort out and we'll be in my room. And you can wipe that satisfied look off your face while you're at it."

Angie shouted something after him, but Hope couldn't hear.

"Damn kid," Cash said as he reentered the bedroom and closed the door. "Thirteen and she thinks she knows it all. Advice on my love life."

Hope's heart skipped a beat. Love life? Was there one?

"Okay," he said, and sat beside her. To her surprise, he reached out and took her hand. "I'm a chicken. That's established. Now we need to establish your right to ask for anything you want. I may not always agree, but damn it, you'd better ask. I *need* to know what you want and need."

She didn't answer immediately. She hadn't been raised to be bold that way, and she was still a little astonished at herself.

"Promise me, Hope. Before we go any further. Will you tell me whenever you're not happy, whenever you need something, whenever you want something? Because I'm not a mind reader, and one of the things that bugs me about what happened with Sandy is that it came out of the blue. I never had a chance to make a course correction or fix anything. So I need to be sure you won't be swallowing things and building resentments."

She nodded slowly. "I think I can do that. I seem to have already started."

He gave her a half smile. "You have. Keep it up. Believe me, it doesn't bother me at all."

"Okay."

"Now. I don't want you to leave. Far from it. I've been so worried that you would that I was breaking things off in advance. Kind of stupid, I guess."

"Kind of understandable," she retorted. "You look at me and see someone who had a gilded life before she came here. I can understand why you'd think I would never be happy any other way. But the thing is, I look back and realize I was never *really* happy before. Oh, a few occasions were great, but overall… Well, Cash, it was never about me. It was about what everyone else wanted from me. I got used to it, accepted it, but since I've been here I've learned that I matter, too."

"You definitely do. More than you may realize. I've got a daughter ready to kill me if you leave. Your happiness sure as hell matters to her. And frankly, it does to me, too. That's why I've been pulling back. How could you possibly be happy here? With me. With the ranch. It's not an easy life."

"No, it's not. I suppose it gets harder at times than I've seen. But the thing is?" She dared to look at him and saw him nod encouragingly. "The thing is, everything I do here seems important and useful. Of course it won't always be easy or happy. But it's still important and useful."

His smile widened a hair. "I want one more promise."

"What?"

"That if you ever can't stand it here, you let me know. Give me a chance to fix it, or at least give you a break."

"Oh, that's easy," she said, her spirits beginning to rise to new heights. "Ask me something hard."

"All right." He drew a deep breath. "I've been running from the fact that I'm in love with you, and I couldn't see how you could possibly be the same. But if you think we can make this work, I want to marry you and raise your child as my own, and maybe have a couple more. Can you handle that?"

Her heart nearly stopped. She could feel her eyes widening, her mouth sagging open. She had never dreamed...

"Okay, too fast. But I want us married before this baby comes, unless you don't want to marry me at all."

Fast? *Fast* was an understatement. All she had asked for was a chance to prove herself here, and now he was proposing? But as the reality of it sank in, she felt as if she were soaring, leaping to the heavens, receiving a happiness greater than she had ever known.

"I'll marry you tomorrow," she said without hesitation. "I love you, Cash. I didn't want to face it, but the whole reason I was thinking of leaving was because it hurt so much to watch you withdraw. I couldn't stand the feeling that I was making you miserable."

"I was making myself miserable. That stops right

now. As for marrying you tomorrow…could we wait a week or two? I'd like to get the church, and some friends, and a little bit of celebration…"

But he stopped. "All I want is you," he said, reaching for her. "You, and your baby, and your smile in my life."

He pulled her close, kissing her in that gentle way of his. Desire ignited within her, and all she wanted was to fall back with him and rediscover all the joys he had taught her.

Except there was a knock on the door.

"Angie, I told you!"

The door opened a crack. "I think I deserve to know. Am I getting a stepmother?"

"Yes."

Angie's whoop of joy filled the house. "And a kid sister, I hope. Well, a boy is okay. Can I come in? I realize you probably want to do the nasty, but there's time for that later."

Hope started giggling. Even Cash started laughing. "Group hug?" he suggested.

The three of them wound up together sitting on the bed, hugging tightly. When the baby kicked, Angie felt it.

"It's going to be a pain," she said with a satisfied grin. "I can't hardly wait."

Hope realized she couldn't wait, either. Not for any of it, because all of it was the rest of her life.

Joy had replaced sorrow and fear, and for the first time in her entire life, she knew the true meaning of home.

* * * * *

MILLS & BOON®

Cherish™

EXPERIENCE THE ULTIMATE RUSH OF FALLING IN LOVE

0315/23